Ethan saw Hannah illuminated in the glow of his headlights, standing still as a statue.

For one wild moment he thought about going back and telling her everything. It would feel so good to unburden himself to someone willing to listen. And he sensed Hannah was the sort of woman who would withhold judgment until the bitter end. But then the moment passed, and he knew that it was best if he went home. Alone.

For these past few days he'd actually allowed himself to pretend that none of the horror of the past had been real. He'd almost begun to feel like every other young widower, playing with his son, laughing, eating, sleeping—even allowing himself to consider a future.

Now it was time for a reality check.

He lived under a cloud of suspicion, and would until the mystery of his wife's death was solved. Until that time, he had no right to drag someone as special as Hannah Brennan into his own particular hell.

Dear Reader,

Once again, Silhouette Intimate Moments has a month's worth of fabulous reading for you. Start by picking up *Wanted,* the second in Ruth Langan's suspenseful DEVIL'S COVE miniseries. This small town is full of secrets, and this top-selling author knows how to keep readers turning the pages.

We have more terrific miniseries. Kathleen Creighton continues STARRS OF THE WEST with *An Order of Protection,* featuring a protective hero every reader will want to have on her side. In *Joint Forces,* Catherine Mann continues WINGMEN WARRIORS with Tag's long-awaited story. Seems Tag and his wife are also awaiting something: the unexpected arrival of another child. Carla Cassidy takes us back to CHEROKEE CORNERS in *Manhunt.* There's a serial killer on the loose, and only the heroine's visions can help catch him—but will she be in time to save the hero? *Against the Wall* is the next SPECIAL OPS title from Lyn Stone, a welcome addition to the line when she's not also writing for Harlequin Historicals. Finally, you knew her as Anne Avery, also in Harlequin Historicals, but now she's Anne Woodard, and in *Dead Aim* she proves she knows just what contemporary readers want.

Enjoy them all—and come back next month, when Silhouette Intimate Moments brings you even more of the best and most exciting romance reading around.

Yours,

Leslie J. Wainger
Executive Editor

Please address questions and book requests to:
Silhouette Reader Service
U.S.: 3010 Walden Ave., P.O. Box 1325, Buffalo, NY 14269
Canadian: P.O. Box 609, Fort Erie, Ont. L2A 5X3

RUTH LANGAN
Wanted

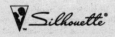

INTIMATE MOMENTS™

Published by Silhouette Books

America's Publisher of Contemporary Romance

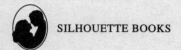 SILHOUETTE BOOKS

ISBN 0-373-27361-4

WANTED

Copyright © 2004 by Ruth Ryan Langan

RUTH LANGAN

is an award-winning and bestselling author. Her books have been finalists for the Romance Writers of America's (RWA) RITA® Award. Over the years, she has given dozens of print, radio and TV interviews, including *Good Morning America* and *CNN News,* and has been quoted in such diverse publications as *The Wall Street Journal, Cosmopolitan* and *The Detroit Free Press.* Married to her childhood sweetheart, she has raised five children and lives in Michigan, the state where she was born and raised. Ruth enjoys hearing from her readers. Letters can be sent via e-mail to ryanlangan@aol.com or via her Web site at www.ryanlangan.com.

Here's to second chances at love.

And of course for Tom. My first and only.

Prologue

Devil's Cove, Michigan—1997

Hannah Brennan's beat-up Ford was loaded with college textbooks, assorted shelves, plastic containers and a duffel bag bulging with dirty clothes. When she reached the outskirts of Devil's Cove, she brought the car to a halt and felt her heart give a little hitch.

The town of Devil's Cove had a checkered past. It had been home to pirates in the seventeenth century, horse thieves in the eighteenth and just plain thieves in the nineteenth. There were rumors that bootleggers had used the coves hidden along the jagged shoreline to transfer illegal whiskey during Prohibition. Though the sleepy little town had become a fashionable resort frequented by wealthy tourists, there was still an undercurrent of mystery, which shimmered like the mist that hovered over Lake Michigan at dusk and tingled along the spine when fog rolled in before daybreak.

It was, Hannah thought, the only place she would ever want to be. But for the first time in her life, that knowledge gave her no pleasure. Devil's Cove, she thought, had been aptly named, at least this day. As she put the car into gear and started toward home, she was feeling like the devil for what she was about to do.

Home to Hannah, her parents and her three sisters was The Willows, a lovely old waterfront home that belonged to her grandparents, affectionately called Poppie and Bert by their granddaughters. Poppie was retired federal judge Frank Brennan and Bert was his wife, Alberta, a much-loved English teacher at Devil's Cove High School. Despite the presence of four adults and four children under one roof, their sprawling house never seemed crowded. There was always room for another classmate, dinner companion, neighbor, as well as the dozens of stray pets Hannah's sister, Emily, managed to bring home through the years.

Hannah maneuvered the car up the curving driveway. Instead of going inside she hurried around to the backyard, skirting the patio and heading toward the garden where she could see her grandfather already hard at work on the hobby that consumed him.

"Well." Frank Brennan looked up from the row of tomatoes he'd been vigorously working with a hoe. "Here's my girl. I was hoping you'd get home in time to give me a hand."

Hannah kissed her grandfather's cheek before picking up a shovel. "You're losing your touch, Poppie. This edge is looking pretty ragged."

"Weeds. The bane of my existence." He grinned, and chopped at a dandelion before tossing it into a basket. "I'm afraid my garden was sadly in need of your touch, Hannah, darlin'."

The two worked in companionable silence for several minutes before Frank turned to Hannah. "How did you do on your exams?"

"Aced them, I think." She stepped the shovel deep into the dirt and turned the soil before moving on.

"Of course you did. I've been boasting to all

my friends about having a granddaughter follow me into the law,'' Frank chuckled. "My son Christopher isn't the only one to exert a little influence around here. Not that it isn't grand that Emily is following her dad into medicine. But now it's my turn. With your excellent grades, I doubt you'll have any trouble getting into the University of Michigan's law school, especially since I'm on their list of distinguished alumni.''

Hannah's shovel bit into sod, and she gave the handle a harder twist than necessary to loosen it.

Her grandfather paused to wipe an arm across his brow. "Hot today. They're predicting a hotter than average summer. These babies are going to need a little extra care if they're going to survive.''

"I'll see that they make it, Poppie.'' She spoke his name with deep affection. "I'll spend the summer pampering your gardens.''

Frank glanced over. "That might be hard to do with the job I've got lined up for you in Lansing.''

Her shovel was forgotten. "About that job in the state capitol…''

He smiled. "I figured it couldn't hurt for you to spend the summer working for one of my fellow judges on the bench.''

"But I..."

"Sorry I spoiled the surprise by telling you before you left school. I'd intended to wait until you got home, but I just couldn't keep it to myself." He caught the frown line between her brows and touched a hand to her shoulder. "I hope you don't mind my intrusion, Hannah. I know I should have waited until your exams were over before making these arrangements. Maybe you'd rather not start working right away, especially since you'll be so far away from home all summer."

"It isn't the distance. It's just..."

They both looked up as the Brennan housekeeper, Trudy Carpenter, approached them with a pitcher of lemonade and two glasses. "Miss Bert said you're to take a break and get out of the sun, Judge."

As wide as she was tall, with hair the texture of cotton balls and a voice like a rusty hinge from a lifetime of smoking, Trudy was a fixture at The Willows, having cooked and cleaned for Frank Brennan and his wife for more than forty years.

"Thanks, Trudy." While she poured, he winked at his granddaughter. "Look who's home from college."

"I noticed." Trudy handed Hannah a sweaty

glass. "She didn't even take time to say hello before dashing out to give you a hand with your gardening. Seems like this old garden is more important than the folks living here."

Hannah kissed the older woman's cheek. "I was planning on coming inside in a little while."

"Uh-huh." Trudy gave a snort of laughter. "You don't fool me, Hannah Brennan. I think you'd rather work in this garden than eat or sleep."

The housekeeper eyed the long-handled contraption lying next to Frank's foot. "I see you gave up on that gadget you spent the winter tinkering with. What're you calling it?"

"The handi-hoe." The old man gave an embarrassed shrug. "It seems to be in need of a bit more work. But once I get the kinks out, it's going to revolutionize gardening."

"Uh-huh." Trudy rolled her eyes as she walked away.

Ordinarily that look would have sent Hannah into spasms of giggles, since the housekeeper had a running feud with Frank Brennan over his inventions. But today Hannah was oddly silent as Frank led the way toward a wooden bench set under the gnarled branches of a giant oak. The silence dragged on as they settled themselves and sipped lemonade.

When their glasses were empty, Frank set his aside and turned to Hannah. ''Now, about that job. If you'd rather not go to Lansing right away, I'll understand.''

''Oh, Poppie.''

At her sound of distress he caught her hands in his. ''What's wrong, darlin'? What's happened?''

When she said nothing he drew her close and draped an arm around her shoulders. ''You know you can tell me anything, Hannah. If someone's hurt you, I'll…''

She gave a quick shake of her head, sending short blond wisps lifting on the breeze. ''It's not what you think, Poppie. It's just…'' She took a deep breath. ''I don't know how to tell you.''

His heart gave a sudden lurch. ''Just say it. Whatever it is, we'll deal with it together, the way we always have.''

''You know how much I love gardening with you.''

Puzzled, he merely nodded.

''I know how proud you are of my grades, Poppie. And how much you enjoy telling everyone that I'm going to follow you into law. But lately I've been thinking about what I really want.''

''And what would that be?'' He smiled and held up a hand. ''Wait. Don't tell me. Let me guess. You're tall and graceful enough to be a model. Athletic enough to be a professional swimmer or golfer. And bright enough to do anything you set your mind to.''

Hannah laughed. ''Spoken like a true grandfather, without a bit of prejudice.''

''Of course I'm prejudiced. But you know you can do anything you want. So what'll it be, darlin'? An actress? A ballerina?''

''I've been thinking about making my love of gardening a career.''

''Gardening? A career?'' He pulled away to stare at her. ''What kind of job is that for a woman?''

''There aren't men's jobs and women's jobs anymore, Poppie. There are just jobs. And gardening makes me happy.''

''Well…'' He tried to be objective, but it wasn't easy switching gears in midstride. ''Happy is fine. But will it pay the bills? Can you actually make a living gardening?''

She shrugged. ''I'd like to find out. I'm thinking of switching from law at the University of

Michigan to horticulture at Michigan State. It's one of the best in the country."

Before her grandfather could open his mouth, she said, "I know you're a proud alumnus of U of M. I know State's your rival. But I've been giving this a lot of thought, Poppie. While I'm studying, I could get some experience by working for other landscapers in the area."

"Doing what? Laying sod? Driving a tractor?"

She nodded. "Why not? It's what I do now, and everyone thinks it's fine, as long as it's just my hobby. But why shouldn't I make my hobby my career? It's been a dream of mine for as long as I can remember." Her voice trembled with excitement. "I even saw a piece of property that would be perfect for what I want. It's the Goddard farm just outside of town, with rolling hills and a huge old barn. I can already see how it would look with seedlings planted in the fields and acres of greenhouses. I know old Mr. Goddard can't keep on farming for too many more years, and his two sons have left the state. I figure, if I save my money while I finish college, maybe I'll be able to persuade him to sell me some or all of it when I'm ready to get started."

"This doesn't sound spur-of-the-moment to

me. It sounds like you've given this a lot of thought.''

She nodded. ''I know you've always admired my logical mind, Poppie. Now, instead of the law, I'll apply it to business.'' Her voice lowered. ''I know I've let you down. All the way home I've been fretting about how to tell you without hurting you.''

''Hannah.'' He looked indignant. ''You could never disappoint me.''

''But...''

He touched a finger to her mouth to silence her before reaching into his pocket to remove his wallet. Inside he retrieved a picture. ''Do you remember this?''

She studied the faded photo of herself; she was standing beside a pumpkin that dwarfed her. Hannah shot him a look of surprise. ''I haven't seen that picture in years.''

''It was taken when you were in kindergarten. You brought home a tiny unidentified seedling in a half-pint milk carton.''

Hannah was laughing now. ''You and I planted it in your garden, and my mystery seed grew into the biggest pumpkin anyone had ever seen.''

He joined in her laughter. "We called it the pumpkin that ate The Willows."

She sobered. "You wanted to enter it in the state fair, but I couldn't bear to pick it before it was finished growing."

Frank nodded. "That was when I realized that you understood the truth of gardening. It isn't about winning prizes. It's about growing things for the sheer joy of seeing them grow. And enjoying the beauty and nourishment they bring to our lives."

She felt her nerves begin to ease. "Is this your way of saying that you don't mind if I don't go into law?"

He studied the picture before looking over at her. "I would have loved another lawyer in the family. But it was a selfish wish on my part. I wanted someone around who could discuss the latest cases that make the headlines. But gardening…" He shook his head. "I love the idea of sharing my love of gardening with you, Hannah."

"Even if it won't pay the bills?"

"I wouldn't worry about that." He tucked the picture into his wallet before returning it to his pocket. "You're smart and clever and industrious. And when you're ready to make the leap,

I'd be proud to loan you the money for that farm.''

Hannah felt tears spring to her eyes and blinked them away. ''You won't be sorry, Poppie. I'll make you so proud.''

''You always have, darlin'.'' He caught her hands in his and squeezed. ''You always will.''

He sat a moment, watching as she returned to the garden to attack the weeds. In his mind he'd been picturing his sweet Hannah in judicial robes. Now he would have to adjust his vision and see her like this—well-worn denims, a sweaty shirt and calluses on those lovely hands.

He blinked and realized that one important thing remained from his original dream. It was that smile of absolute delight on her face as she worked the soil.

If gardening made her this happy, what right did he have to deny her that dream?

Chapter 1

Ethan Harrison awoke to the sound of a foghorn, and for a moment he thought he was back in Maine. He actually reached across the bed for Elizabeth before the realization struck. This wasn't Maine. He was in his new home in Michigan. And Elizabeth would never share his bed again.

He slipped into a pair of faded shorts and a T-shirt before padding down the hallway to the big room his two young sons shared. Seeing that they were both still asleep, he made his way down the stairs to the kitchen and plugged in the

coffeemaker before rummaging through the cupboards for cereal.

He carried the bowl and spoon out to the big
wooden deck that looked out over Lake Michigan, and settled down on the top step with his
back against the rail. Fog and mist rolled over
him in damp waves, leaving his skin chilled.

The morning was as bleak as his mood. He'd
come to Michigan to get as far away from the
past as possible. But now he realized that the real
lure of this place had been its proximity to water.
If he had to leave everything that was comfortable and familiar, at least he would have some
of it in his new surroundings. Of course, the fact
that Devil's Cove was small and secluded was an
important factor, as well. He wanted, needed desperately, to find a safe haven for his sons.

He'd known the minute he saw this place that
it was exactly what he'd been hoping for. Though
his yard ran right down to the water's edge, a
sandbar just offshore formed a natural barrier,
making it impossible for a boat to get close
enough to come ashore. The fact that this was a
private, gated community, restricting all but those
whose names were posted with a guard, made it
all the better. He'd permitted his real estate agent
to post the names of workers who needed access

to it. All others would require his express approval before being allowed on the premises.

The sweeping grounds, with over an acre of aged trees hiding a tall iron fence, made it appear to be just another millionaire's retreat, though Ethan considered it more of a fortress.

A fortress. The thought added to his gloom. He hated having to lock his sons away from the world, but for now it seemed the only solution.

At the sound of tires crunching on the gravel drive, he looked up to see a truck roll to a stop. Seconds later the truck's door opened and a figure in torn jeans walked to the tailgate and began tugging on a heavy tarp.

Curious, Ethan set aside his empty bowl and strolled over. "Need a hand?"

"Thanks."

At the decidedly feminine voice, he found himself stepping back to stare.

"You work for the contractor?" She kept her back to him as she began retrieving shovels and rakes and tossing them to him.

"Afraid not." He couldn't help admiring her long, long legs and trim backside as he set each tool aside in the grass.

"Oh." She glanced over her shoulder, and he had a quick impression of pale blond hair beneath the baseball cap and eyes the color of honey, before she turned back to her work. "Did Martin hire you?"

"Martin?"

"My crew boss." She retrieved the last of the equipment and brushed her hands down her pants before turning to him. Her smile was absolutely captivating. "Are you a new hire?"

"Sorry. No."

She looked him up and down, considering. "Then what are you doing here at this time of the morning?"

"I live here."

"You live..." She stopped, and her smile turned impish. "Oops. You must be the new owner. I thought you weren't moving in until next week."

"I decided to get an early start. And you'd be..."

"Hannah Brennan." She stuck out her hand. "Hannah's Gardening and Landscape. I was hired to do your yard."

"Ah. Ethan Harrison." He latched on to the only thing that his brain could manage in the presence of that dazzling smile and firm handshake. "Brennan. Are you related to Charlotte, my real estate agent?"

"My mother. But nobody calls her Charlotte. Around here, she's Charley."

"Charley. I'll remember that." His smile widened. "She came highly recommended by an old college friend. I don't know what I'd have done without her."

Hannah nodded. "She's the best."

"I'll say. After only a few questions over the phone, she seemed to know exactly what I had in mind. It only took her a few days to get back to me with a list of several places she wanted me to see. When I flew out here, I expected to spend weeks making a decision. But the minute I saw this place, I knew it was the one."

Hannah looked beyond him to study the house, one of several million-dollar mansions that had recently been built on waterfront acreage that was part of an old orchard. "It's a great place. And this view…" She didn't bother to finish the sentence, allowing the sight of sunlight breaking through the mist over the water to speak for itself.

Ethan nodded. "It was the view that sold me." He didn't bother to mention the security.

He glanced back at the truck. "So you're going to turn this weed patch into lawn and gardens, are you?"

''That's what I do best.'' She smiled. ''I don't have to get started today, though. I didn't realize you'd moved in. You probably have a million things to see to. If you'd like me to schedule another time…''

''No. You certainly won't be in my way. I think it'll be fun to watch the lawn and gardens take shape and…''

At the peals of laughter, Hannah turned toward the deck in time to see two little boys dressed in pajamas barreling down the steps and launching themselves into their father's arms.

Ethan caught the two in a bear hug and swung them around before setting them on their bare feet in the grass. ''T.J., Danny. This is Hannah Brennan.''

Hannah knelt down and offered her handshake. The older of the two stuck out his hand.

''Are you T.J. or Danny?''

''Danny.''

''Hi, Danny. How old are you?''

''I'm four.'' He held up four fingers.

''So old? And what about your little brother?''

He grinned and pointed to the toddler holding tightly to his father's ankle. ''T.J.'s two.''

''Two,'' the little boy echoed.

''What does T.J. stand for?''

"Thaddeus Joseph," Danny said proudly, causing his little brother to grin widely.

"That's quite a mouthful for such a little guy. No wonder you call him T.J."

"Uh-huh. Daddy says I'm a big boy."

"It's nice to be a big brother."

"Do you have one?"

Hannah shook her head. "Just sisters. I have a big sister and two little sisters."

"Do you have to watch out for them when they're playing?"

"I did when they were younger. Now they're big enough to look out for themselves."

He eyed her truck. "Is that yours?"

"Yeah." She got to her feet. "Do you like it?"

He nodded. "It's bigger'n Daddy's car."

"Is it?" She glanced over at Ethan and winked. "Well, he only has to haul two little boys around, but I have to haul a crew of workers, as well as a lot of tools."

"Wow." The little boy eyed her with respect. "You work with tools?"

"Shovels. Rakes. Trenchers. Tractors."

"Tractors?" Danny turned to his father with a shriek of delight. "Can I watch the tractors?"

Ethan got down on one knee. "You can. As

long as you and T.J. stay on the deck, where you'll be safe. Tractors can be fun to watch, but they can be deadly if the driver can't see you." He glanced over his son's head. "Danny has been in love with trucks and tractors since he was a baby. In fact, he has an entire construction yard ready to be set up in his bedroom. If we can find which box it's in."

Hannah looked impressed. "I'd like to see that sometime, Danny."

"Can I show her, Daddy?"

Ethan nodded. "I don't see why not. Another time. Right now I think we'd better get inside and I'll fix the two of you some breakfast."

His little son turned to look at Hannah. "Are you going to drive a tractor here today?"

"Not for a couple of days." She slipped off her baseball cap and ran a hand through her hair. "Today I'm just going to do a walk-around and decide where everything will go. Then, after your daddy approves my design sketches, I'll get my crew started."

"One day will you come inside and see my trucks?"

"I'd like that." She grinned at the younger boy, who clung to his father's leg.

As the two little boys scampered toward the

house, Ethan turned back. "I think I'd better warn you. Now that Danny has found someone who drives a truck and a tractor, he may become something of a pest. Whenever he gets in the way, just let me know."

Hannah gave a shake of her head, sending blond wisps dancing. "I wouldn't worry about it. It's sort of flattering to find a guy who isn't put off by the fact that I drive a truck."

She turned away and busied herself folding the tarp. Minutes later she heard the door slam and the peals of laughter from the kitchen, which told her that father and sons were enjoying their breakfast.

While Hannah and her crew chief completed their inspection of the yard, Hannah made crude sketches on a clipboard.

"Ground cover in that shady area." She pointed with her pencil. "And I'm thinking maybe a perennial garden over there."

Martin Cross nodded his agreement. "What about those old forsythia and lilac?"

Hannah shrugged. "I don't want to tear out anything more than necessary. Part of the charm of this property are the mature plants left over from its former life. But if they prove to be more deadwood than blooms, we'll have to yank them.''

''I'll take some cuttings and see what I find.''

''Thanks, Martin.'' Hannah paused beneath an ancient oak. The gnarled, twisted limbs lent a dignified beauty to the yard, despite the fact that the ground beneath was too densely shaded to allow any grass to grow.

She walked around the spot, mulling over ways to improve the lawn while sparing the tree.

Martin held his silence while she added to her sketches. When she stuck the pencil behind her ear, he dug the keys from his pocket. ''If we're through here, I'll join the crew on the Anderson job.''

Hannah nodded absently. ''I'll run my ideas past my client and get over there as soon as I can.''

''No hurry.'' Martin sauntered toward his truck. ''I told the sod farm we wouldn't be ready for delivery until noon. I got the crew started on leveling the dirt before I left.''

Hannah glanced at the sun, which had already burned away the fog. ''I'd feel a lot better if we could get that sod down before dark. The sooner it's down, the sooner I can get the sprinklers started.''

"Will do. If I have to, I'll pull the crew from the Richardson job to lend a hand."

Hannah waved as he drove away, then climbed the steps and knocked. From inside she could hear the wail of sirens and the high-pitched sound of children's voices.

After a few minutes she knocked again, louder, and peered through the screen.

Seeing no one, she opened the door and called, "Hello."

When she received no answer, she stepped inside and cupped her hands to her mouth. "Hello. Anybody here?"

The silly question had her chuckling. It was obvious to anyone within a mile of here that somebody was home. The voices and the sirens were much louder now and coming from upstairs.

She followed the sound and paused at the foot of the stairs to shout, "Hello up there. Can anybody hear me?"

A minute later, two little faces were peering down at her.

Danny gave a squeal of delight. "We're playing firemen." He waved a fireman's hat and pointed to the fire truck that was wailing. "Want to come up and play?"

"Sorry, I can't. But I'd like to check some things with your father. Is he around?"

"He's up here."

"Would you tell him…" She heard the patter of feet as the two boys disappeared from view.

While she was still wondering what to do, Ethan appeared at the top of the stairs. "I apologize. I didn't hear you over all the noise up here." He started down the steps, his two sons trailing behind.

Hannah couldn't help smiling at the sight of the two little boys, hair slicked from their showers, wearing shorts and matching shirts with an image of a bulldozer on front. Each one carried identical hard hats with a fire-engine logo.

"I've made some preliminary sketches of your yard, but I hate bothering you with this now. Why don't I leave them with you, and you can call me after you've settled in."

Ethan was already shaking his head. "Thanks to your mother, the settling in part was easy. At my request, she arranged for beds and bedding, dishes in the cupboards, hangers in the closets. In fact, she even put food in the refrigerator. The only thing we had to do was show up."

"Even with all that, I doubt it could be an easy move with two little boys."

He shrugged. "We're doing fine. Now, why don't you tell me what you're thinking of doing with the yard?"

"All right." She led the way outside, with Ethan and his sons following behind.

Half an hour later, when they had circled the property, Hannah removed her sketches from the clipboard and handed them to Ethan. "I'm sure you'll want to take your time looking these over. When you're ready, you can call me and we'll discuss any changes you might want me to make."

He accepted them and studied the drawings. "Did you study art?"

She shook her head. "That's my sister Sidney's department."

"She's an artist?"

"Wildlife, mainly. She has a place in the woods so she can be close to nature. You'll see her posters of waterfowl in shops and galleries all over town."

"I'll look for them. I think I'd like some for the boys' room. T.J. is crazy about ducks." He glanced at her sketches. "But these aren't too shabby, either. You have a good eye."

"For flower beds," she laughed. "That's the extent of my artistic talent."

"It looks good to me." He looked up. "Ever think about doing this on a laptop instead of paper and pen?"

She shrugged. "Too complicated. I just carry my clipboard everywhere."

Ethan considered for a moment, then said, "Okay. Whenever you and your crew are ready, you can get started."

"Just like that? You don't want to take some time to think about it?"

"I don't need time." He looked up and met her eyes. "I know when I see something I like."

The look in his eyes sent tiny pinpricks of electricity along her spine. Despite the heat, she actually shivered.

"Well, then." She turned away, feeling heat stain her cheeks. "I guess we can start in a couple of days."

She was startled when a small hand tugged on hers. "When you come back, will you be bringing your tractor?"

"Yes. And if your daddy says it's all right, I'll even let you and your brother sit on it." She squeezed his hand. "Goodbye, Danny. Goodbye, T.J."

As Hannah drove away, the sight of Ethan and his sons had the smile returning to her lips. While the youngest boy watched from behind his father's legs, his four-year-old brother was dancing around them like a tiny wind-up toy. The look on his face was one of pure joy.

Chapter 2

Hannah stepped from the shower and wrapped her hair in a towel before sinking gratefully into the whirlpool tub. With a sigh she leaned back, eyes closed, as the jets pulsed warm, fragrant water over her protesting muscles. After hours of working alongside her crew laying sod, this felt like pure bliss.

The first thing she'd done after buying this property from old Mr. Goddard—a local cherry farmer eager to retire to Florida—was to remodel the loft above the barn for an apartment. The former dark, dreary storage room was now a bright, cheery space, thanks to whitewashed wood and

the addition of several skylights. The bathroom
was decidedly feminine with pale, unglazed tile
on the floor and walls, and bright touches of color
in the pots of flowers that bloomed everywhere.
Her sister, Sidney, had painted vines and flowers
around the skylights, and added whimsical fairies
flitting here and there across clouds painted on
the ceiling.

The barn hadn't been her only consideration.
Before investing in this location, she'd carefully
tested the soil to be sure that it would support
the growth of the various seedlings that now pa-
raded in neat rows across the hillside. And
though she'd already built half a dozen greenhouses, abloom with flowers she'd grown from
seed, she planned on doubling that number in the
next couple of years.

Hannah stepped out of the tub and toweled
herself off before walking to the adjoining bedroom. A headboard of bent twigs and a matching
chaise were covered in pale-ivory linen. The
room-size rug resembled a garden, holding more
flowers. Pots and vases of them were everywhere.
And a scattering of Sidney's vines and fairies
painted along the arched door that led to a balcony, where flowers seemed to fill every available space outdoors, spilling out of giant urns and

tumbling over the railing, cascading all the way to a stone patio below.

Hannah's cats, a lop-eared old gray-and-white named Tiger and a pretty orange-and-white tabby named Marmalade, were stalking butterflies across the balcony. Their antics made her stop and laugh before she slipped into a pair of gauzy slacks and a matching top the color of raspberry sherbet.

"Someday you're going to catch one of those beautiful butterflies, and you won't know what to do with it."

The two cats paused long enough to slant her a look before returning to their game.

She slid her feet into sandals, then ran a brush through her damp hair. Except for a touch of color on her lashes and lips, she had no need for makeup. Though she wore sunblock and never worked outdoors without a cap, she couldn't entirely avoid the sun. Her skin seemed perpetually bronzed by it.

"Good night, you two." She gave each of her pets a gentle scratch behind their ears before grabbing the keys to her Mercedes convertible.

Though she was comfortable driving a truck with her crew, she'd bought the little car to indulge her love of speed and freedom. There was just something about feeling the wind in her hair that made these gentle summer nights so special to her.

Of course, she thought as she danced down the stairs, got into the car and started it, summer was special for another reason. She loved her work. So much so, she was almost embarrassed to be making so much money doing something that gave her such pleasure.

The day she had repaid her grandfather his loan, exactly one year to the day, had been a proud one for her. The fact that he was equally proud added to her pleasure. He hadn't simply supported her decision to take on this career; he had enthusiastically embraced it, recommending her to everyone he knew. Thanks to his connections and word of mouth, she had more work than she could handle.

As she drove through town toward The Willows, she found herself wishing she hadn't promised her grandmother that she'd come to dinner. It would be fun to drive out into the country, turn the car loose on the hilly curves and stop for a hot dog and thick shake at the Dairy Devil.

There would always be another night, she consoled herself. Tonight she would enjoy the fun and laughter that always seemed so much a part of the Brennan family affairs. Whether a simple barbecue on the patio or a formal meal in the dining room, her family needed no one except each other to add flavor and spice. The Brennans had both in abundance.

She turned up the curving driveway of The Willows and sat for a moment, soaking up the feelings of love that always came over her at the sight of this faded old mansion. Like the town, it owned her heart. With a light step, she bounded from the car. She breathed in the wonderful fragrance of home-baked rolls as she walked into the front foyer. Hearing voices on the patio, she hurried along a hallway and paused in the doorway of the kitchen.

"Are those cheese rolls?"

Trudy Carpenter straightened, tossed aside an oven mitt and turned. "Your favorites, Hannah."

"You never forget."

"'Course not." Though Trudy claimed to have no favorites among the Brennan girls, she had a particular soft spot for this little tomboy who had grown up into a rare beauty. She'd grieved along with the entire family when Hannah's father, Chris, had died the previous year. And now, though the four sisters had moved out of their grandparents' big home, they all lived just minutes away in town. Close enough to visit often.

"Here you are." Charley Brennan strolled into the kitchen and embraced her daughter before picking up a pitcher of lemonade.

The two women walked outside to the patio where the rest of the family had gathered.

Charley circled the table filling glasses. "I hear you met Ethan Harrison and his sons today."

Hannah trailed behind her, pausing to brush a kiss over her grandmother's cheek and hugging her grandfather. "Yeah," Hannah laughed. "I sort of barged in on him this morning without bothering to call first. I was hoping to do my walk-around before he moved in. I hope he didn't call you to complain."

Charley gave a shake of her head. "Not at all. He wasn't bothered by you. In fact, I had the impression he was rather charmed."

"Yeah. That's our Hannah." Courtney looked up from a side table where she was filling a plate with some of Trudy's fabulous Creole shrimp appetizers. "Always charming the customers."

"I do my best." Hannah reached over her sister's shoulder and helped herself to a shrimp.

Sidney, standing beside her grandfather, wrinkled her nose. ''I hope you weren't wearing that ratty old pair of denims you seem to favor these days.''

''As a matter of fact, I was. In case you've forgotten, I'm required to get down and dirty when I work.''

''Which is,'' her brother-in-law, Jason Cooper, said with a wink, ''extremely sexy from a guy's point of view.''

Hannah brushed a kiss over his cheek before turning to her sister Emily, who was holding his hand. ''Now I see another reason why you married him. He has excellent taste.''

''Even if he does have very poor eyesight,'' Courtney added with a laugh.

The others joined in the laughter as they began to take their places around the table. Trudy arrived, pushing a trolley laden with domed silver platters.

As she lifted the lid of the first platter and offered some to the judge, he studied it with a look of suspicion. ''Fish again?''

''Not just any fish. Fresh Norwegian salmon.''

''So you say. But I know that you and Bert have conspired to get me to eat health food.'' At the housekeeper's pained expression, he sniffed, then helped himself to a generous portion.

"You might want to leave some for the rest of the family," she said in an aside as she moved past him.

The others merely grinned and rolled their eyes. Frank Brennan and Trudy Carpenter had been carrying on a running argument for more than forty years, though neither would admit it. But beneath the well-chosen taunts lay a deep well of affection.

As they helped themselves to salmon and a lovely salad of beefsteak tomatoes and hearts of palm, Charley turned to her daughter. "What did you think of Ethan Harrison?"

"He's certainly decisive."

"What does that mean?"

"He barely looked at my drawings before giving me the approval to get started."

Courtney giggled behind her hand. "Maybe he was dazzled by your charm."

"Or your fabulous taste in clothes," Sidney added with a laugh.

"Or it might be—" Frank winked at Hannah "—that your drawings showed him exactly what he was seeing in his own mind."

"I hope so." She reached for a cheese roll in a napkin-lined basket. "Because I intend to get started tomorrow."

"So soon?" Her grandfather seemed surprised.

"The crew I was planning to send to the Carter house has been freed up because the brick for that project hasn't arrived yet. So I figure I'll get them started on some of the hardscape now, re-arranging boulders and shoring up a retaining wall. And I'll deal with the plantings and lawn whenever I have some time."

Charley helped herself to more lemonade. "What did you think of the house?"

"I didn't see much of the inside. But the setting's gorgeous. Once we remove a couple of dead trees, it'll offer an unobstructed view of the lake."

Courtney nudged Sidney. "Forget the house. What we want to know is what you thought of its mysterious owner."

"Mysterious?" Hannah glanced from one sister to the other. "What's that supposed to mean?"

When they didn't answer, she turned to her mother. "Do you know anything about Ethan Harrison?"

"Very little." Charley smiled. "He's the father of two little boys. He wanted to be near the water and he seemed especially interested in safety and privacy. He didn't want to move in without at least a few basic necessities already in place, so I arranged it.''

Hannah nodded. ''He was thrilled with all that you did for him, Mom. He said you took care of the beds and linens, and even the food in the cupboards.''

Bert touched a hand to her daughter-in-law's arm. ''That's why you're the best in the business, my dear. There seems to be no request too outrageous for you to handle.''

''I didn't mind, Bert. Especially since this man was coming all the way from Maine, with two little boys. He said he and his sons would be driving in as soon as he could clear his business schedule.''

Hannah arched a brow. ''What is his business?''

''He and his partner founded a software company. That's about all I know. Since money seems to be no object, I assume he must be awfully successful at what he does.''

''What about a wife?'' Hannah seemed to take more time than usual buttering her roll and avoiding eye contact with her mother.

''I gather he's a single father. But whether it was because of death or divorce, I can't say.''

Courtney wasn't fooled by her sister's feigned disinterest. "Do I detect a bit more curiosity than usual over this particular newcomer to our town?"

"Don't be silly." Hannah set down her knife with a clatter. "You know I make it a point to never date a client."

"So you say." Courtney grinned at her sister, Sidney, across the table. "But there's always a first time." She waited a beat before asking, "So, what does this client look like?"

Hannah shrugged. "Tall. Sandy hair. Really unusual eyes."

"You mean the color?" Sidney, always the artist, was trying to paint a picture in her mind.

"Not the color. They're hazel. Nice enough color, I guess." Hannah fiddled with her fork. "But it's the way he looks at you. It's…really intense."

"Intense, hmm? Slim? Stocky? Fat?" Courtney knew she was pushing, but it was her nature to get as much as she could from the usually tight-lipped Hannah.

Hannah shook her head. "Trim. Works out, I'd say."

"You mean he has a great bod?" Courtney's grin deepened.

"I guess so. I didn't really notice." Hannah turned, avoiding the glint in her sister's eyes. "He's really great with his kids."

"Uh-huh. Let's see." Sidney shared a laugh with Courtney. "Tall. Great body. Intense, hazel eyes. Maybe next time you ought to pay more attention, Hannah."

Around the table, the entire family, including Hannah, burst into gales of laughter.

"Okay," she admitted. "So maybe I did notice. It's hard not to. But that doesn't mean I'm going to act on it."

"That's my girl." Frank Brennan leaned over to pat his granddaughter's hand. "One wedding this year is quite enough, thank you."

That had Jason Cooper looking over to tease the old man. "Oh, I don't know about that. You and I are still outnumbered around here. I think it'd be nice to add a couple more guys to the mix. And this one comes with sons."

That had the others laughing.

Hannah's food was suddenly forgotten. As the conversation swirled around her, she thought about the man she'd met that morning. She'd felt an instant attraction. But because she had a rule about keeping her clients at a distance, she'd deliberately denied the feeling, especially since she hadn't known whether or not he had a wife.

Now she was going to have to work overtime to pretend she didn't notice him. Not a problem, she told herself. After all, she wouldn't have to see Ethan Harrison and his sons for more than a few weeks, and even then, only from a distance. After that, her job would be done and she could walk away.

Satisfied that she'd taken care of that minor problem, she put him out of her mind before helping herself to some salmon.

Chapter 3

"Thanks, Martin." Hannah leaned into the open window of the truck to speak to her crew boss, who had delivered a load of boulders. "I'll stay with this crew and you can finish up at the Andersons'."

"We should be through there by supper time." Martin motioned with his thumb: "I'll come back with the hauler and help you load up before dark. Unless you'd rather leave the equipment here overnight."

She thought a minute. "Let me check with my client. If he doesn't object, I'd just as soon keep everything here until we're finished."

"Right." Martin waved his cell phone. "Call me later."

Hannah nodded before turning away. She'd kept a crew of half a dozen to help with this job, while Martin took the rest with him.

She pointed to the side of the yard that sloped toward the water as she called to the men, "We're going to start with that retaining wall. Those old rotted timbers need to be removed before we can set the stones in place and start planting."

While several workers began hauling the timbers aside, Hannah settled herself on a tractor and began scooping up the discarded timbers and depositing them into the back of a stake truck. Within minutes she caught sight of Ethan and his sons watching and waving from the top step of the deck. She waved back, then drove across the yard and left the tractor idling as she jumped to the ground and crossed to them.

Danny danced down the steps to greet her. "Hi, Hannah. You brought your tractor."

"You bet." She ruffled his hair before smiling up at his little brother, who was clinging to his father's ankle. "I hope we didn't wake you."

Ethan shook his head. "We were awake. We just weren't out of bed yet."

"That's 'cause Daddy was telling us silly stories." Danny started giggling. "He tells the best stories. Especially if we promise to scratch his back."

Hannah arched a brow. "You mean you have to bribe him?"

The little boy turned to his father. "What's *bribe?*"

"It means you do something nice for me, so I'll do something you want."

"Oh." The little boy's eyes rounded. "But Daddy tells silly stories even if we don't scratch his back. And sometimes he even lets us eat our cereal and drink our juice in his bed."

"That's one very brave daddy you have," Hannah laughed. "My father threatened to ground us for a week if we ever dared to leave crumbs in his bed."

"What's *ground?*"

Hannah's laughter deepened. "That's something you won't have to learn for a couple more years. And then you'll probably become very familiar with it." She looked up at Ethan, who remained on the top step with his youngest son, who was eyeing the tractor. "If you'd like, we could arrange to start much later from now on so there's no chance of waking you."

Ethan shook his head. "That's not necessary. But I hope you won't mind having us hanging around watching for the next few days. The minute the boys heard the sound of that tractor, I knew it was useless to try to keep them indoors."

"Maybe they'd like to go for a ride before I get back to work?"

The two little boys started dancing around their father. While Danny shouted, "Ride! Ride!" his little brother echoed, "Wide! Wide!"

Ethan nodded. "Okay. But I think I'd better go along and hold T.J."

He swung the little boy into his arms and followed, Danny racing ahead beside Hannah. She climbed up to the seat and settled Danny on her lap before sliding over to make room for Ethan and T.J. When they were all settled, she put the tractor in gear and allowed the two little boys to grip the steering wheel. With her hands just beneath theirs, she managed to steer without appearing to.

"Look, Daddy. I'm driving. I'm driving."

Danny was shouting above the sound of the engine, while his little brother merely giggled with glee and called, "Diving. Diving."

"You're doing a good job, little buddy." Behind his son's back Ethan winked at Hannah, and she wondered at the way her heart took a funny little dip.

"Hold on, now." She turned the wheel slightly to avoid the pile of boulders, and the two boys gave whoops of excitement as their little hands appeared to be doing the job.

"Did you see that, Daddy?"

"I did. You're getting really good at that." Ethan bent to nuzzle his youngest son. "And you. Driving just like a big boy."

Little T.J. beamed with pride.

"All right now." Hannah pointed to the porch. "I think after our tour of the yard, it's time our drivers took us over there. How about it?"

Both Danny and T.J. gripped the wheel tightly as she brought the tractor to a gradual stop.

"Okay, boys. Time to let Hannah get back to work. What do you say to her?"

"Thank you, Hannah." Danny's face was wreathed in smiles.

T.J., clearly delighted, managed to lisp, "Tank you, Hannah."

"You're welcome." She helped Danny down, and waited until he and his father and little brother had climbed the steps before putting the tractor into gear and backing away. "If you'd like, we'll do it again later in the day."

That brought a chorus of cheers from the two little boys.

With a wave of her hand she returned to her work. Whenever she looked over at the porch, she caught sight of Ethan and his sons watching. It was nothing new to Hannah to have clients watching as she and her crew worked. She understood the fascination people had with tractors and lawn equipment as they darted back and forth making drastic changes in the landscape. She not only understood, but had also learned to be comfortable with an audience. This time, however, there was something definitely distracting about Ethan Harrison.

At first she told herself it was because of what she'd heard last night. The mystery man. Where was his wife? Was he a widower or divorced? Not knowing enough about him was causing her a bit of discomfort. But there was something else going on here. She'd felt a sizzle along her spine when his hip had brushed hers during their tractor ride. Though she'd told herself it was nothing, she'd felt it again when his shoulder rubbed against hers. No more than a tiny pinprick of heat, but it had been enough to have her sweating. She had been greatly relieved when the ride was over and she could turn away from him. But even then she'd had the distinct impression that he was staring holes through her back.

He had the most direct stare she'd ever seen. A way of pinning her with those eyes. What was even more disconcerting was the way his lips seemed to curve upward, as though he'd just thought of something particularly amusing each time he looked at her.

She wiped sweat from her eyes and forced herself to concentrate on the task at hand. But as she hauled yet another load of rotten timbers toward the truck, she caught sight of Ethan standing in the doorway and calling to his young sons, who were just turning away.

Both boys were laughing at something their father had said, and she found herself charmed by the fact that he seemed so adored by his sons.

She recalled her sisters' teasing. How could a man like Ethan Harrison ever be considered something of a mystery?

Not her business. And it was time, she reminded herself sternly, that she immersed herself in the business at hand.

"Okay. Who's got the ham and cheese?" Hannah set down a box from the local sandwich shop and began rummaging through it, tossing wrapped bundles to the men who were sprawled in the shade of a giant oak.

"That's mine," called Bret, a burly young football player with a shaved head.

Half the team from Devil's Cove High School vied for jobs with Hannah's crew during their summer break. The pay was good and the hard, physical work was just what their coach encouraged to keep their bodies toned.

"Tuna on rye?" She glanced around before tossing another, then read the label of a third with a growing smile. "Did somebody here actually order peanut butter and jelly?"

The entire crew howled as a blond, freckled football player raised his hand. In defense he shouted, "Hey. Knock it off. My mom taught me that pbj was good for me."

"Boy, did she have you conned," one of the older guys said as he bit into his second hot dog. "It never occurred to you that she said that because it was easier to make than anything else?"

The kid had a blank look for a moment before he ducked his head.

"That's all right, Kevin." Hannah stretched out beside him and began unwrapping her own lunch. "My mom tried that line on me, too. And

I believed it until I was, oh…six or seven, anyway.''

That brought another round of laughter from the crew.

''Hey, Hannah.'' Bret nudged the guys on either side of him. ''What do you eat to keep that girlish figure? Sprouts and watercress?''

''In your dreams, Bret.'' She bit into a thick burger dripping with melted cheese and chili. ''I'd rather keep up my energy and let you worry about my girlish figure.''

While the others roared with laughter, she looked up to see Ethan and his boys standing over her. She felt her cheeks grow hot, and was grateful when Ethan held up a six-pack of soda, deflecting attention away from her.

''I saw that you'd stopped for lunch and figured you'd enjoy this.'' As he passed around the frosty cans, Danny and T.J. plunked themselves down in the grass on either side of Hannah.

''Did you two have lunch?'' she asked.

Danny nodded. ''Daddy made us peanut butter and jelly.''

That brought another round of laughter from the crew.

''I bet he told you it was good for you,'' Hannah said with a straight face.

"Uh-huh." Danny pointed to the plastic bottle of water resting at her hip. "Don't you drink soda?"

"Not while I'm working. I can't deal with the sugar buzz. I prefer plain old water."

Ethan nodded toward the pile of boulders. "Think you'll be able to get all those in place before dark?"

"That'd be nice, but I don't think it's possible. We've probably got another couple of days on this project." Hannah polished off the last of her burger and washed it down with a long drink of water. As she capped the bottle she glanced at the two little boys. "How about another tractor ride before we get back to work?"

The two were up and dashing toward the tractor as soon as the words were out of her mouth.

She turned to Ethan. "I guess that's a yes."

As he strolled along beside her he couldn't help laughing. "You certainly know how to make two little boys happy."

"It's easy. I work with guys all day. After a while it becomes second nature."

"I doubt your crew would be happy with a simple tractor ride."

"You'd be surprised at how little it takes to

keep them happy. A sunny day, a good lunch and a fat paycheck.''

''And what does it take to keep their boss happy?''

She glanced over to see him watching her. Again that odd little tingle. She decided to keep it light. ''Pretty much the same. I'm a sucker for a sunny summer day.''

She pulled herself up to the seat of the tractor and helped Danny settle himself onto her lap. Ethan lifted little T.J. into his arms and sat beside her. Minutes later they were circling the back-yard, moving slowly around the pile of boulders and debris from their morning chores.

Above the noise of the engine, Ethan said, ''I can't help noticing how much you seem to love your work.''

She nodded. ''I wouldn't trade with anybody.''

''That's one of life's great gifts. I hope you appreciate it.''

''Oh, I do.'' Hannah glanced at her watch. ''We'll take another turn around the yard. My guys deserve a little more time to relax before I start cracking the whip.''

Danny looked over his shoulder with big eyes. ''You have a whip?''

She broke into laughter. "Not exactly. But I let them think I do."

"They don't look like they're afraid of you," he said matter-of-factly. "They like you, Hannah."

"Now how would you know that?"

He shrugged. "I could just tell, 'cause they were all laughing and easy with you when we walked up."

"Yeah. They were." She ruffled his hair. "I guess I'll have to come up with something else besides a whip to keep them in line, huh?"

The little boy merely grinned and returned his attention to the steering wheel of the tractor. With little yelps of pleasure, Danny and T.J. continued holding tightly to the wheel until Hannah brought it to a stop near the porch.

"Thanks, Hannah." Danny scrambled down and ran a hand lovingly over the big tires. His little brother followed his example and did the same.

Ethan touched a hand to hers. "I'll add my thanks, too. I haven't seen them this excited in a long time."

"It's nothing. Really." She wondered at the heat that raced up her arm.

"Maybe it's nothing to you. But it's a really big deal to them. And to me. Thanks again."

He stepped down and scooped up the two boys, carrying them to the top of the steps where they turned and waved.

Hannah returned the wave before backing up the tractor and heading toward the retaining wall, where her crew had already begun the tedious task of removing the last of the timbers.

The heat of Ethan's touch remained, she realized. Warmer even than the heat of the sun.

Not a problem, she reminded herself. A couple of weeks and she'd move on to the next job, the next client.

Still, she had to admit that having a client as sexy as Ethan Harrison added a little spice to the job.

Chapter 4

"That's it for today, guys." Hannah tipped up her water bottle and drained it before glancing at her watch. "Just hang here a minute and I'll see if the client wants us to clear the equipment." She crossed the big yard and climbed the steps. Before she could knock, the door was thrown open and she stared down at two little faces peering up at her. "Hi, Danny, T.J. Is your daddy around?"

"In here." Ethan turned from the stove. "Come on in."

"Sorry. I'm too dirty." Hannah remained on the deck. "I just wondered if I could leave the equipment here overnight. We'll cover it with tarps. It won't be pretty, but it's a lot easier than hauling it away every night and returning it every morning.''

Ethan walked over to stand behind his two boys, who were holding the door open. ''Of course you can leave it. We're not planning any garden parties.'' He grinned at his two sons. ''Are we?''

Danny looked up at his father. ''What's a garden party?''

Ethan shrugged. ''Just what it sounds like. A party in the garden. And since our gardens haven't been planted yet, it's too soon to have one.'' He turned to Hannah. ''There's no need to cover the equipment. In fact, I know two little boys who are itching to climb up and sit on that tractor the minute you and your crew are gone. That is, if you don't mind.''

Hannah laughed. ''Be my guest. But just to make sure they don't get carried away, I'll take the keys with me.''

''What's the matter? Afraid I might be tempted to drive it while you're gone?''

Hannah gave Ethan a slow appraisal. Despite the casual shorts and T-shirt and the faded leather sandals, he couldn't hide his prep-school manner.

Maybe it was the razor-short hair, or the tanned and perfectly toned body that spoke of hours in the gym. "Somehow I just can't picture you being comfortable on a tractor."

"I'll have you know I worked on a cement crew my freshman year in college." His grin was quick and deadly. "My first day on the job I dragged my hide home, aching in places I never even knew I had. I was so tired I never even made it to bed. I fell asleep right inside the doorway of my bedroom."

He shared a laugh with Hannah before adding, "And by the end of that summer I vowed I'd find an easier way to make a living."

Hannah glanced around for emphasis. "It looks like you did."

"Yeah. One year on a cement crew was enough motivation." Hearing the timer on the stove, he turned away. "Time to start the rotisserie. I'm fixing chicken. Want to join us?"

Hannah glanced down at her stained denims and muddy work boots. "I'd love to. But I need to scrub off a day's worth of grime before I can even think about dinner."

"You've got time. The chicken won't be ready for at least an hour."

"Sorry, but I..."

She was shaking her head and backing away when Danny caught her hand. ''Please, Hannah. You said you'd come up and see my construction yard.''

''I don't think...'' She saw the flash of disappointment in his eyes and hesitated. Beside him, little T.J. mirrored his brother's sadness.

That was all she needed to cave in.

She turned to Ethan. ''If you're sure it's no trouble?''

''No trouble at all.'' He fiddled with the dials on the stove before turning to give her a smile. ''How about six-thirty?''

She glanced at her watch and nodded. ''Okay.'' She winked at Danny and T.J. ''See you then.''

She could hear the two little boys actually cheering as she stepped off the porch and crossed to her waiting crew. The sound stayed with her as she and the others secured their equipment with tarps before climbing into trucks and taking their leave. By the time she'd arrived home to strip off her filthy clothes and soak away the dirt of the day, she'd come to the conclusion that those two little boys must be terribly lonely to show such a reaction to something as casual as a last-minute dinner guest.

* * *

Hannah stepped out of her car and picked up the little handled bag from the wine shop before starting toward the porch. Even before she'd started up the steps the door was opened and the two little boys came tumbling out to greet her.

"Wow." Danny caught sight of the red convertible, and his smile turned into an ear-to-ear grin. "Look, Daddy."

Ethan stepped to the door. While the two boys raced past Hannah to study her car, he stopped in his tracks and simply stared. Gone was the ever-present baseball cap. In its place was hair as shiny as corn silk that had him itching to run his hands through it. She was wearing simple white jeans and a white eyelet blouse tied at her midriff, which showed off her sun-kissed skin to its best advantage. On her feet were white sandals. And he noted her bare toes sported a coat of pale-pink polish that looked freshly applied.

When he found his voice he managed to say, "You clean up really good."

"Thanks." She dimpled and handed him the bag. "I stopped at the wine shop. I hope you like Pinot Grigio."

"If you like it, I'll love it." Hearing his sons' squeals he looked over. Seeing the car, he arched a brow. "No truck tonight?"

"That's for work. When I'm on my own time I prefer something hot."

He chuckled, then called, "Danny, T.J. I don't think Hannah will appreciate your fingerprints on the door of her hot wheels."

Danny's eyes were as big as saucers by the time he'd returned to the porch. "T.J. and I have Hot Wheels, too, Hannah."

"You do? I hope you'll show them to me."

"Can we, Daddy?"

Ethan nodded. "If you'd like, you can take her upstairs right now."

"Come on." Danny raced ahead, with T.J.'s little legs pumping hard to keep up.

Ethan stood watching as Hannah followed at a more leisurely pace. It took him a moment to realize that she'd disappeared up the stairs, and he was standing completely still holding the bottle of wine. With a shake of his head he went off in search of a corkscrew.

A short time later he climbed the stairs and paused in the doorway to his sons' room. T.J. was holding up a racing flag, while Danny and Hannah knelt side by side at the starting gate of a miniature car raceway. When T.J. lowered the flag, two tiny cars were released from their gates and went careening down a plastic hill and around several curves before rolling to a stop at the finish line.

''I won.'' Danny was jumping up and down. ''I won, Hannah.''

''Yes, you did.'' She hugged him before turning to his little brother. ''Now the winner gets to race against the challenger. This time I'll hold the flag. Come on, T.J. Which car do you want?''

The little boy took his time before choosing a candy-apple-red car and placing it at the starting gate, beside Danny's blue one.

''Did you pick that color because of my car?'' Hannah asked him.

He smiled shyly before nodding his head.

When Hannah lowered the flag, the cars again rolled down the hill and around the curves before coming to a stop at the finish line.

''Uh-oh.'' Hannah walked over to study the cars before looking up. ''I think this one's a tie.''

''Can we go again?''

Hannah nodded toward Ethan. ''You'll have to ask your father if there's time for one more.''

Danny turned. ''Do we have to go eat now, Daddy?''

''We do unless you'd like your chicken burned to a crisp.'' Ethan handed Hannah a stemmed glass of white wine. "Did you guys show Hannah your tractors?"

"Yeah. She knew the names of all our stuff, Daddy." Proud of his newly acquired knowledge, Danny walked around the room where he and Hannah had arranged a mock construction yard. "This one's a backhoe. And this is a Bobcat. And this one's—" he paused and turned to Hannah "—I forgot this one."

"A front-end loader."

"Oh, yeah. 'Cause the scoop is in the front, right, Hannah?"

"That's right."

Ethan gave a shake of his head. "I'm impressed."

"You should be." Hannah arched a brow. "How many women do you know who can rattle off the names of heavy equipment?"

"I can't think of one."

"There you are."

"Hannah said she's been to real auto races, Daddy."

Ethan's smile grew. "Why am I not surprised?" He turned toward the doorway. "Come on, boys. Let's take Hannah downstairs now and feed her."

He waited until she walked past him, then

trailed slowly behind. The view of her backside as she descended the stairs had his throat going dry. There was, he had to admit, no prettier sight in the world than a tall, tanned goddess in snug-fitting white jeans.

Hannah looked around the kitchen. "Want me to set the table?"

Ethan shook his head. "I've decided the evening is too good to waste indoors. I thought we'd eat on the deck."

He led the way outside, where hurricane candles flickered on a round glass table set for four. A simple galvanized bucket of ice held the bottle of wine, as well as a plastic pitcher of lemonade.

"Oh." Hannah breathed in the familiar scent of water and moist earth. "Is there anything sweeter than a summer evening in Michigan?"

"I can't think of one. Have you lived here all your life?"

She nodded, then remembering her manners, turned. "Would you like me to help carry out the food?"

"I'll handle it." As he turned away, Ethan called to his sons, "Show Hannah where you'd like her to sit."

"You sit here, Hannah." Danny indicated a

swivel chair. "That way you're between T.J. and me. Daddy always sits there." He pointed.

"All right." Hannah took her seat and watched as the two little boys scrambled into their chairs. "Would you like me to pour you both some lemonade? Or do you prefer milk?"

"Lemonade, please." Danny watched as she filled his glass.

"T.J.?" Hannah turned, and the little boy nodded and held his glass as his big brother had done.

Ethan carried a platter to the table. Besides the chicken, there were tiny potatoes roasted with garden vegetables and a basket of rolls.

"Oh, that looks wonderful." Hannah sipped her wine and watched as Ethan placed a small amount on each of his son's plates before holding the platter out to her.

She helped herself to chicken and vegetables. Seeing T.J. struggling with his food she asked, "Would you like some help?"

He nodded so she reached over to cut his chicken and vegetables into tiny bites. When she'd finished buttering his roll, he smiled his gratitude before he began to eat.

"How about you, Danny? Need any help?"

"No, thanks," he told her. "I'm a big boy."

"Right. I forgot."

Across the table Ethan watched in silence.

After just one taste Hannah sighed. "Oh, this is much better than the cold pizza that was going to be my dinner tonight."

Ethan gave a dry laugh. "Thanks, I think. Does this mean my cooking is only marginally better than last night's leftovers?"

She smiled. "You might say that. But if I'm going to be honest, I'll have to admit that this is wonderful." She winked at Danny, then at T.J. "Your daddy is a really good cook."

Danny emptied his glass and wiped his mouth on the back of his hand. "Are you a good cook, too, Hannah?"

"If I'm in the mood. I have a couple of favorite recipes that I like to play with from time to time. But most days I'm just too tired and dirty to care what I eat, as long as it's protein and carbs."

"What's protein and carbs?" he asked.

"Meat. Cheese. Pasta. And lots and lots of gooey fat. That's what fuels me."

"You mean like gasoline?"

She laughed. "Sort of. I burn a lot of energy in my work and I've discovered that I need to replace it on a daily basis or I get grumpy."

"Is that like sad?"

She nodded. "Something like that."

The little boy glanced at his father. "Daddy gets sad sometimes."

Hannah saw Ethan's quick frown before he ducked his head. "We all get sad sometimes." She turned to include T.J. in the conversation. "That just makes the happy times even better. It's like seeing storm clouds roll away, leaving the sky filled with sunshine."

The two little boys seemed to think about that for a moment before returning their attention to their food.

Across the table Ethan picked up his wine. Over the rim of the glass he studied the woman who was laughing and chatting so easily with his sons. Her good humor was contagious.

He decided to relax and simply enjoy the moment. There'd been too few of them in recent memory.

Chapter 5

"More wine?" Ethan reached toward the bottle in the ice bucket.

Hannah shook her head. "No, thanks. I've had enough."

She eyed the frozen confection-on-a-stick being enjoyed by Danny and T.J. "But I'll have one of those if you have more."

Ethan arched a brow even while his mouth curved into a grin. "What flavor?"

She considered a moment before saying, "Cherry if you have it. Otherwise I'll take anything."

"I'll see what's left." He went inside and returned minutes later with two cherry Popsicles. When he saw her look of surprise he shrugged. "I didn't want to be the only holdout." He motioned toward the steps. "Let's walk around the yard and see what you and your crew accomplished today."

With the boys skipping along ahead of them, Hannah and Ethan trailed more slowly.

She pointed to a shady area. "I know I didn't pencil anything in for this spot, but I think in time you should consider building a playscape there."

"Why?" He liked the sound of her voice. It was, he decided, a happy, friendly voice. Even on the phone, without ever seeing her face, he would know he was talking to someone with a boundless enthusiasm for life.

"That area gets no sunlight. I could plant ground cover, but the smarter thing to do would be to cover the ground with mulch to soften any falls and build some activities for the boys. For now, while they're little, some swings and a slide. As they get older, maybe a climbing wall or tower."

"Why didn't you draw that into the plans?"

"Honestly?" She glanced over with a sly grin.

"I didn't want to overwhelm you with too many projects. Not to mention the added expense."

She could see that he was considering the idea so she decided to push ahead. "Another reason for the playscape is to deter Danny and T.J. from wandering too close to the water."

He nodded. "I hadn't thought of that."

She polished off the last of her flavored ice and licked at a drop of cherry juice that trickled down her chin. At once she became aware of the fact that Ethan was staring at her in that quiet, intense way she'd noticed.

Because she needed to fill the silence, she asked, "Can they swim?"

Ethan shook his head, momentarily distracted. "Don't you think they're a bit young for that?"

"When you live this close to the water, there's no such thing as too young to swim. You should realize that there's just something about water that attracts kids. They need to know how to save their own lives if they should ever find themselves in over their heads."

"Yeah. I'd forgotten that. I grew up on the water, and the temptation to jump in over my head got me in more than a few scrapes." He gave her an admiring look. "I'm glad we had this talk. I think I'd better phone the YMCA tomorrow and ask about lessons.''

Hannah nodded as the boys came racing toward them. ''That's what I'd do.'' As an afterthought she added, ''Years ago, when I was in high school, I taught a swimming class at the Y. They have some really good instructors.''

''You're a good swimmer?''

She shrugged. ''Not bad. Growing up in Devil's Cove, we were all water babies. Devil's Cove High School has an awesome swim team.''

''Can we go swimming, Daddy?''

At Danny's excited question, Ethan nodded. ''One day soon. What do you think about taking swimming lessons?''

''Oh, boy.'' The minute Danny began to dance around, his little brother got caught up in the excitement and did the same.

Ethan winked. ''That was easy.'' He paused beside a wild growth of iris and tall grass that more nearly resembled a jungle than a garden. ''This wasn't in your plan, either. What do you propose we do with this?''

''I thought you might want to save it. I see it as the perfect spot for a rock garden, after we get the rest of the yard in shape. The rocks are already there. They've just been buried beneath all those old plants. Look at them.'' Her tone became almost reverent. ''Coneflower. Heliopsis. Sage. Autumn Joy. As for this mass of iris plants, I'll dig them up and separate the rhizomes, so they can grow new stalks. I think it's nice to have some older gardens to soften the look of a new yard. With a little work, this could be really healthy.''

Danny, who had crouched down to peer through the jungle, looked up at Hannah with wide eyes. ''Do you know the names of all of these?''

''Just about all.''

''Are you a plant doctor, too?''

She laughed. ''I guess I am. I haven't yet met a sick old plant that I can't turn into a thing of beauty.''

''Is that 'cause you love them?''

She knelt down beside him and reached toward a giant bearded iris bent nearly double from the weight of the blossom. ''How could I help but love something this beautiful?''

He studied the golden bloom with a slightly darker honey-colored center, before his smile widened. ''It's almost the same color as your eyes.''

''Is it?'' She looked at the flower, then back

at him. "Maybe that's why I like it so much. Did you know that when I was just your age, I was already working in the gardens with Poppie."

"Who's Poppie?" the little boy asked.

Hannah settled down on a low stone wall that was badly in need of repair. "Poppie is my grandfather. We call my grandmother Bert, because her real name is Alberta. My family lived with my grandparents in their big house just down the way. You can see the roof from here." She pointed, and both Danny and T.J. turned to follow her direction, where the last rays of sunlight glanced off the highest peaks shingled in dull gray.

"Did you ever play here?"

At Danny's question she nodded. "When I was little, this was a cherry orchard. My sisters and I used to slip over here when the cherries were ripe and eat all we could pick. Then we'd go home and complain about the way our tummies ached, and Poppie would say, 'You've been sneaking into Mr. Wardlow's orchard again.'"

"Was he mad at you?"

"Not really. Poppie understood the lure of ripe cherries. I wouldn't be surprised if he helped himself to a few in his day."

"Did he take you to the doctor?"

Hannah shook her head. "My father was the town doctor. His clinic was in the back of the house."

Danny looked at her in horror. "Did you have to get lots of shots?"

"No more than you, I bet. But it was really nice to know that we never had to make an appointment to see the doctor. We could see him any time we wanted."

"Was your Poppie a doctor, too?"

"He was a judge. He's retired now and still working in his gardens. But he believes his true calling is as an inventor."

Danny and T.J. settled themselves on either side of her. Though T.J. still allowed his older brother to do all the talking, he was quickly losing his fear of this stranger as he moved close enough to breathe in the soft summer fragrance that seemed to cling to her.

"What's an inventor?" Danny asked.

"Someone who makes something really useful that we never even knew we needed." She laughed. "Poppie has made garden tools which, unfortunately, never seem to work as well as he'd hoped. And kitchen utensils, which only add to the chores of our already overworked housekeeper. Her name is Trudy Carpenter, and she's been around since I was your age.'' She tapped an index finger on T.J.'s nose, which caused the little boy to giggle.

''Can we meet Poppie and Bert and Trudy someday?'' Danny asked.

Hannah nodded. ''I know they'd love to meet both of you. It's been a long time since they had little people around to play with. Bert was a wonderful teacher. And Trudy adores children. She bakes the best cookies in the world, which is why Poppie is constantly adding inches to his waistline. I think he'd be willing to share some with you, though. He's very generous with people he likes.''

''Do you think he'd like us?''

''He'd love you.''

Pleased, Danny caught her hand. ''Come on, Hannah. Show us the rest of the work you did today.''

With Danny holding one hand and T.J. imitating him by catching her other hand, the boys led her away, with Ethan trailing behind.

They paused when they reached the area where the crew had been working all day.

''I wanted to start with the retaining wall.'' Hannah pointed. ''That way, you wouldn't have to look at the pile of boulders for more than a week or so.''

''Your crew does good work.'' Ethan watched as Danny and T.J. left her to climb to the top of the tallest boulder, where they did their best to balance before toppling into the dirt.

Hannah nodded. ''They're a good group. The younger ones are on the high school football team, and they consider this a good way to stay in shape for the season. Plus, they get to work on their tans so they can impress the girls.''

Ethan chuckled. ''Another bonus is that they get to work alongside a real babe all day long.''

''A babe?'' Because he'd caught her by surprise, she found herself blushing before she managed to turn it into a joke. ''Yeah. Right. More like their pain-in-the-neck slave driver. After a day of sweating and rolling in the dirt, there's no way they'd ever see me as an object of lust.''

He tipped up her chin. ''If you believe that, lady, you're wearing blinders.''

Though he'd intended it to be humorous, the minute he touched her, everything changed. He felt a quick flash of need so sharp, so strong, he had to bank the urge to crush her against him and kiss her senseless. Because he hadn't felt this way in such a long time, he was startled by the intensity of his feelings.

Catching the light of surprise in her eyes, he gave her a smoldering look. ''You, Hannah Brennan, are the sexiest slave driver I've ever met.'' Like his son, he leaned close and breathed her in before stepping back and lowering his hand to his side.

She waited a moment for her heart to settle, wondering if the ground beneath had actually tilted. Or had she just imagined it?

Because she was flustered by the feelings that rippled through her, she was actually grateful when Danny and T.J. came rushing up to cause a distraction.

''Is that old tree dead?'' Danny pointed to a gnarled oak with a trunk so big, it would have taken half a dozen arms to span it. The roots had grown through the soil and snaked along the ground like giant, twisted ropes.

''Not at all.'' She walked closer, eager to put some distance between herself and the man who was making her so uncomfortable. ''It just takes a while for older trees to get their leaves.'' She studied the sturdy branches that soared several stories into the air. ''To me, a tree like this is something magical and wonderful.''

"Magic?" Danny's interest was immediately piqued.

"Maybe not real magic. But think how old it must be. I bet it was alive before my Poppie was born. Think of all the wonderful things it has seen in its day." She studied the old tree. "I think this would make a grand tree house when you two get a little bigger."

"A tree house? Oh boy, Daddy. Can we have one?"

At Danny's shriek of excitement, T.J. ran to his father and tugged on his hand.

Ethan looked down at his little boy and laughed. "I think Hannah is putting way too many ideas in your heads tonight. Swimming lessons. Playscapes. And now a tree house. In a magical tree, at that."

"Can we, Daddy?"

"We'll see."

"That's the classic line of every parent." Hannah knelt down and said in a stage whisper to Danny and T.J., "'We'll see' can mean anything from 'not on your life' to 'here's hoping if I delay long enough, they'll forget all about it.'"

"Guilty," Ethan laughed. "I hope this doesn't mean you're going to reveal all my secrets to these two."

"I wouldn't dream of it." Hannah got to her feet and pointed to the tractor. "I don't have the key with me, but if you'd like, you can still climb aboard and pretend to drive it."

That was all the encouragement the little boys needed. With shouting and laughter filling the air, they pulled themselves up to the seat of the tractor and wrapped chubby hands around the wheel, making engine sounds as they did.

Danny stood up and waved. "Daddy. Hannah. Come on. We'll take you for a ride."

Hannah and Ethan climbed up to the seat and settled the boys on their laps.

Hannah brushed a wisp of blond hair from T.J.'s cheek. "I was just about your age the first time Poppie let me sit on his lap and drive the lawn tractor. That was all it took to get me hooked. While my sisters were playing with dolls, or reading books in the hammock, all I wanted to do was work with Poppie."

"Was it hard?" Danny asked.

"It probably was, but I never thought so. When you're doing what you love and spending all your time with someone you adore, how can it feel like work? I thought Poppie was the smartest man in the world. He knew the names of all the flowers. Even the wildflowers that grew in the woods. He would take me for walks and point out the plants that were safe to eat, and the ones that would make me sick. I can't tell you the number of times he picked a mint and urged me to chew the leaves, or to taste the sweet nectar of a clover. I'm sure my friends thought it was strange that I wanted to spend so much time with an old man, working all summer hoeing vegetables and hauling water in sprinkling cans that weighed almost as much as I did. But I wouldn't trade a single minute of it.''

She pointed to the orange ball of sunlight that seemed to be sinking beneath the distant shore. ''Look. Poppie used to say there wasn't a prettier sight in all the world than the sun setting over Lake Michigan.''

T.J. yawned and rubbed his little fists over his eyes.

Seeing it, Hannah turned to Ethan. ''I think all this fresh air has someone ready for bed.''

Danny sat up straighter on his father's lap. ''I'm not tired, Daddy. Do I have to go to bed, too?''

With a laugh, Hannah reached over to tousle his hair. ''I wasn't talking about you. I'm the one who needs to get to bed.''

Danny caught her hand. ''Will you come upstairs first and tell us another story about Poppie?''

Ethan gave a shake of his head. ''Another time, Danny. Right now I need to get your little brother into the tub and off to bed before he falls asleep right here. As for Hannah, she's put in a long day. She needs her sleep, too, if you want her to show up for work again tomorrow.''

''Will you be here tomorrow, Hannah?''

She was touched by Danny's eagerness. ''I certainly will.''

She waited until Ethan climbed down from the tractor before handing T.J. over to him. The little boy wrapped his arms around Ethan's neck and pressed his face against his father's shoulder.

Hannah felt a quick, hard tug at her heart before turning toward her car. When she settled herself inside, Ethan stood with his younger son in his arms and his four-year-old clinging to his hand.

She gave them all a warm smile. ''Thank you for dinner. I had a really great time.''

Ethan returned her smile. ''So did I, Hannah. And I know my boys did, too. Good night.''

As she turned the key in the ignition, she couldn't resist calling to Danny and T.J. ''If

you're awake in time tomorrow, we'll start the
day with a real tractor ride."

Danny gave an excited shout while his little
brother merely closed his eyes and yawned.

With a wave of her hand, Hannah put the car
in gear and drove away.

Ethan started toward the house.

Beside him, Danny was chattering happily.
"That was fun, Daddy. I wish we had a Poppie
like Hannah. It would be fun to have a grandpa
who knew everything."

"Yes, it would." He climbed the steps and
waited until his son was inside before heading
toward the upstairs. "I think we'll have to do
really quick baths tonight before heading off to
bed. What do you say?"

"Yeah." Danny stifled a yawn. "I want to get
to sleep as fast as I can, so I can be up in time
to drive the tractor in the morning."

All the while that Ethan helped his sons get
ready for bed, he marveled at their good humor.
Without a word of protest, they climbed into their
beds and snuggled under their blankets. By the
time he'd kissed them good-night and stepped
from the room, their breathing was slow and
easy, signaling that they were already on their
way to dreamland.

In his own room he paused at the window to stare down at the moonlight glistening on the water. Strange, he thought, that one person filled with a zest for life had brought them more simple joy in one evening than they'd enjoyed in years.

It hadn't hurt that she was so easy to look at. But beauty, even as rare as Hannah's, wasn't enough. He knew plenty of beautiful women who would have been completely bored with an evening spent in the company of two little boys. Hannah Brennan had not only seemed delighted by them, but had used her considerable charm to put them at ease.

His sons weren't the only ones eager for morning to come. There was no denying the fact that he couldn't wait to see her again.

Chapter 6

"Daddy." Little Danny had his nose pressed to the glass, watching as Hannah's truck rolled to a stop in the driveway. "Hannah's here. Hannah's here."

Ethan turned away from the stove and strolled to the window to stand beside his two sons. He understood their eagerness. He was feeling like a kid himself this morning. His first thought had been that Hannah would soon be here, bringing her own particular brand of sunshine.

When she stepped from the truck and started across the yard, he felt his heart do a crazy dance in his chest. She had a loose-limbed way of walking. Like a dancer, but instead of a leotard, she was dressed in snug-fitting jeans and a T-shirt that read For This I Went to College? Little wisps of hair had already slipped from beneath her bright-yellow baseball cap.

"Hannah. Hi." Danny was shouting at the top of his lungs as he and T.J. ran to her.

"Hi, yourself. I see you're up early today." She got down on her knees to give them both a hug.

She was just straightening when Ethan came strolling up. He may have hidden his excitement better than his sons, following at a more leisurely pace. He found himself thinking that it would have been much easier to be a little boy she'd willingly hug than a man she merely smiled at. But one look at that glorious smile of hers that started at her lips and spread to those honey eyes, and he could feel all his cool control melting away.

"Morning, Ethan. It looks like I have two eager helpers today."

"They've been watching for you for half an hour."

"Such a long time." She held up the keys to the tractor. "Then we'd better not keep you waiting another minute."

Danny and T.J. ran ahead and had already climbed to the seat of the tractor when Hannah and Ethan got there.

Hannah lifted Danny to her lap and made room for Ethan and T.J. beside her. She turned the key in the ignition and the tractor engine roared to life, causing the two little boys to clap their hands in delight.

"All right, you two." Hannah waited until they'd curled their fingers around the wheel before engaging the gear. "Time for a tour of the yard."

As the tractor rumbled in a slow circle, the two little boys tugged on the steering wheel while filling the air with little yelps of excitement. It never seemed to occur to them that Hannah was actually controlling the vehicle.

When they'd made a complete turn, Hannah could see that they weren't nearly ready for it to end. "How about another tour, guys?"

Two little heads bobbed in agreement, and she winked at their father as she nudged the tractor into another slow arc.

Ethan listened to the high-pitched laughter of two little boys and thought it the greatest sound he'd ever heard. There had been a time when he'd wondered if any of them would ever again remember how to laugh. They'd lived under a dark cloud for so long now, he'd forgotten just how glorious a light heart and a little bit of happiness could feel.

When at last they came to a stop at the porch and climbed down, Ethan stood between his two sons. "How do you think we ought to thank Hannah for that ride, boys?"

Danny's eyes lit up. "We could make her breakfast."

"Sorry." Hannah was laughing as she adjusted her baseball cap. "I've already had breakfast, Danny."

For a minute he looked crestfallen. Then he said, "We could make you lunch."

"That's very generous of you, Danny. But I usually send one of my crew for lunch. We flip a coin to see who gets to take a break for that chore. If you were to feed me, you'd have to feed half a dozen hungry guys, as well."

"What about after work?" He turned to his father. "Could we feed Hannah dinner again?"

Ethan nodded. "I don't see why not. It's the least we can do."

"There's no need for that." Hannah was already shaking her head. "You don't owe me din-

ner every time I take a few minutes to play. I
had as much fun as the rest of you.''

"Even so, we'd like to make dinner.''

She thought a minute. "I've got a better idea.
There's a place up in the hills, not too far outside
town, that makes the thickest shakes and the juic-
iest foot-long hot dogs in the world. I've had a
craving for them for days now. If you'd like, you
could pick me up at my place after I've had time
to shower, and that'll save you having to cook.''

Ethan looked down at his two sons. "What do
you two think?''

"I love hot dogs.'' Danny gave a quick nod
of his head and T.J. followed suit.

"Sounds like a plan.'' Ethan grinned. "You
can give me directions to your place before you
leave today.''

Hannah waved her hand before turning the
tractor toward the pile of rocks on the far side of
the yard, where her crew had already assembled
for another day of work.

"Yes, Mason.'' Ethan balanced the phone between his ear and shoulder, and spoke to the
gatehouse guard while loading the breakfast
dishes into the dishwasher. After listening to the
voice at the other end of the line, he paused.

"Sorry. I didn't realize she was flying in today or I'd have given you her name in advance. Of course you have my permission to allow Ms. Crain access."

Minutes later he stepped out onto the deck and watched as a car rolled to a stop beside Hannah's truck. A dark-haired woman strode toward him carrying a leather attaché case.

She glanced around at the mounds of dirt and rocks that littered the yard, and had to shout over the noise of the heavy equipment. "For this you left Maine?"

He chuckled and escorted her inside, closing the door against the noise. "Hi, Selena. You know you didn't have to make this trip. You could have sent everything via messenger."

"I know. But I wanted to see for myself just where you'd decided to hibernate." She wrinkled her nose. "This is even worse than I'd expected."

"You're seeing it at its worst. Once the landscaping is completed, this place is going to be beautiful. Look at that view of the lake. And the town of Devil's Cove is really quite charming."

"I drove through it on my way here." She gave a mock shudder. "All those quaint little gift shops and tourist attractions. I can't imagine actually living here.'' She gave him a long, level look. ''Please tell me this is just a summer place, and you aren't considering anything permanent.''

He shrugged. ''I've learned to take things one day at a time. For now the boys and I are feeling calm.''

''But are you happy?''

Again that shrug. ''Right now I'll settle for calm.''

She frowned. ''Different strokes. But where does that leave our company, Ethan?''

''That hasn't changed. We're still partners, Selena.''

''Not if you had your way. But I'm holding firm on my decision not to buy you out.''

When he opened his mouth to interrupt, she held up a hand. ''We're still a good team, Ethan. You're the computer whiz who can design any kind of program and I'm the one with the head for business. We've built a multimillion-dollar operation out of a dream. We're going to stay together and see this through.''

''My reputation is costing us clients, and you know it.''

''Some. But I'll dig up new clients.''

''This isn't fair to you, Selena. Name your price and I'm gone.''

"And I've told you before. This is just a little bump in the road. Once it's over, we'll move on. Right now the only thing that has changed is your location. You're still able to design the clients' software. I'm still able to negotiate the contracts. Speaking of which…" She opened the attaché case and held up a packet of documents. "There are going to be several changes to the Davis contract." She glanced around. "Is there an office in this place?"

Ethan pointed to the stairway. "Upstairs. But we'd better work here on the kitchen table, so I can keep an eye on the boys."

Selena's gaze skimmed the two little figures standing on the deck and avidly watching the workers. "Where's their nanny?"

Ethan grinned. "You're looking at him."

She grimaced. "At least tell me you have a housekeeper."

"Not yet. But don't worry. I know how much you love gourmet coffee. I'll make a fresh pot and join you in a few minutes. How long can you stay?"

"Only a few hours. My plane leaves at four." As she spread out the documents on the kitchen table she huffed out a breath. "If you have half a brain, you'll book a flight and join me."

* * *

"Daddy." T.J. and Danny raced inside from the deck, where they'd been watching the workers for the past hour. "Hannah's having lunch with the men now. Can we please go out and sit with her?"

"Hannah?" Selena glanced at Ethan.

"Hannah's Landscaping." He turned away from the documents they'd been going over for the past hour and strolled to the window to stand beside his two sons, watching the easy give and take between Hannah and her crew. "Why don't we give her time to relax first?"

"She can relax with us, Daddy. Please. We won't get in the way."

Ethan looked down at the two faces staring up at him with such pleading in their eyes, and relented. They'd been so good, following orders and staying within the safe confines of the deck, even though he could see them twitching with excitement. "Go ahead. I'll bring your lunch out in a few minutes."

Danny and T.J. were out the door before he'd even finished speaking. He watched them sprint across the lawn.

The sight of them had him chuckling before he turned away and began rummaging in the refrigerator. "Okay, Selena. What'll it be? Ham and cheese or peanut butter and jelly?"

"You're kidding." The look on her face was priceless. "Isn't there a place in this town that could deliver something civilized?"

"I suppose so. But I haven't had time to check them out." He began slathering slices of bread with peanut butter and jelly. "State your preference now or go hungry."

She sniffed. "Sorry. I'd rather starve than eat what you're fixing."

"Suit yourself." He pointed to his laptop. "If you'd like to type in those changes, I can initial the revised contracts when I come back inside."

He left his business partner working at the table while he crossed the yard with a tray of sandwiches, sliced fruit and ice-cold juice boxes.

"Sit here, Daddy." Danny scooted over closer to Hannah.

She was reclining in the shade of the big oak, leaning back on her elbows, her long legs extended in front of her. Her feet, crossed at the ankles, were encased in heavy work boots. Her now filthy T-shirt was plastered to her like a second skin. She'd removed her baseball cap, and her hair formed tiny wet curls the color of wheat that stuck to her forehead and neck. She was hot, sweaty and caked with mud. And she absolutely took his breath away.

Ethan greeted her crew before passing out sandwiches to his sons.

Danny took a bite. "Peanut butter and jelly." He turned to the blond, freckled football player who was stretched out with his eyes closed. "Hey, Kevin. My dad made your favorite. Want some?"

The young man sat up, shoving damp hair out of his eyes. "If I hadn't already eaten half a dozen I'd take you up on that. But I don't have room for another bite, squirt."

Danny beamed at his new nickname. "Okay. Maybe tomorrow. My daddy makes the best peanut butter and jelly sandwiches in the world. Don't you, Daddy?"

"You bet." Ethan grinned at the crew. "And I didn't even have to pay him to say that."

That brought a burst of laughter from the others.

Ethan watched as Hannah tipped up her water bottle and drank. "What healthy lunch did you have?"

She grimaced. "You're starting to sound like Bert."

"That's Hannah's grandmother," Danny said casually.

Hannah turned to him with a look of surprise. "I didn't think you'd remember." She shot Ethan a mock-pained expression. "Bert is always forcing healthy food on the rest of us. I think she sees it as her duty to be the family conscience."

Danny set his sandwich aside to pick up the juice box. "What's a conscience?"

"That nagging little voice that tells us right from wrong."

"Is my daddy a conscience, too?"

Hannah saw the sly grins from the others. "That's part of a daddy's job description, Danny. He wouldn't be doing his best if he didn't teach you right from wrong."

"Is that like saying we have to take care of each other? And telling us that good boys don't whine?"

"Exactly. I remember getting that same lecture from my dad. And whining..." She gave a mock shiver. "That was like nails on a blackboard to my dad. All it ever got us was trouble. And a guarantee that we wouldn't get what we wanted."

Hannah looked up as a truck rolled to a stop in the driveway. "Here's my crew chief, Martin

Cross. I'd better see what he needs." As she got to her feet, she paused. "Danny and T.J., would you like to walk with me?"

The two boys caught her hands and danced away, leaving Ethan with her crew.

"Better watch it, Mr. Harrison." Kevin took a long pull on his Gatorade. "I think Hannah's going soft on those kids of yours."

Ethan chuckled. "I'm not surprised. They do have a way of winning hearts."

The teenager watched as Hannah and the boys paused beside Martin's truck. "I wouldn't have thought it of Hannah. She's tougher than any of us. I know guys on my football team who won't work for her because they're afraid she'll embarrass them by working circles around them."

Ethan arched a brow. "That's their loss. Anybody can see that she loves what she's doing."

"That's what I told them." Warming to his subject, Kevin drained the last of the bottle and reached into a cooler for another. "She never asks any of us to do something she wouldn't do herself."

Ethan saw several heads nodding in agreement.

"And she's fair with us." Kevin unscrewed the top of the bottle and chugged. "The day of the prom she sent us all home at noon so we had time to pick up our tuxes and the corsages for our girls. And she paid us for a full day.''

''You sound like a walking ad for Hannah's Landscaping.'' Ethan picked up the empty tray and got to his feet. ''I think when you finish school, you ought to consider a job in public relations, Kevin. Hannah would probably be the first to sign on.''

The others were still laughing when Ethan walked over to claim his sons.

Chapter 7

The day had turned into a scorcher. The temperature hovered in the nineties, and there wasn't the faintest breeze to stir the air. The guys in Hannah's crew had removed their shirts, and once an hour they turned the hose on themselves for some relief while they continued working on the retaining wall.

By three o'clock, when half of the boulders had been positioned, they were dragging.

"It's looking good. But in this heat, we'd better call it a day." Hannah climbed down from the tractor and mopped at her face with a damp towel.

"It'll look even better when we get all the planting done." Martin Cross pointed to the stake truck parked to one side, where a second crew was busy unloading a variety of bushes and flowering plants.

"Hopefully, we'll get at them tomorrow." Hannah tipped up a water bottle and drained it before setting it aside. "See that they're thoroughly watered before your crew leaves, Martin."

He nodded and turned away, calling orders to his crew. While some finished unloading, others began misting the plants, while the remainder of the crew began securing the equipment before heading home.

Hannah removed her baseball cap and ran her fingers through her wet hair as she climbed the steps to the deck. Before she could knock, the door was yanked open, and she found herself staring in openmouthed surprise at a young woman looking cool and composed in a navy linen pantsuit. Her dark hair was perfectly styled in a smooth pageboy. Her makeup was flawless.

"Did you need something?" Selena looked her up and down with an expression of disgust. Her voice was as cool as her manner.

"Oh, hi," Hannah laughed. "I know I'm

filthy. Don't worry. I won't track any dirt inside. I'm looking for Danny and T.J.''

"Whatever for?"

Hannah glanced beyond her. "Are they around?"

"I believe they're upstairs with their father. Could I take a message?"

"Sure. Tell them..." Before she could finish she heard Danny's voice.

"Hannah." Danny squealed with pleasure and raced down the stairs, followed by T.J.

Both were wearing shorts and matching shirts with pictures of cartoon characters. Their hair was still wet from the shower and their feet were bare.

"Oh." She gave a mock sigh. "You guys look so cool. I can't wait to get into the shower."

"Want to use ours?" Danny turned as his father walked up behind him. "Daddy, is it all right if Hannah uses our shower?"

Ethan studied the dirt that streaked her face and had to clench his hands at his sides to keep from touching a finger to the spot. "It's fine with me, but I doubt you could persuade her."

Hannah could feel her cheeks grow hot at the way Ethan was staring at her, and started backing away. "Sorry. This much sand would clog your drains. I'm heading home right now. I just stopped by to let you know I was through working for the day. We had to knock off early because of this heat.''

''Yay. Work's over. Now it's time to play.'' Danny was jumping up and down, and though T.J. didn't quite understand why, he imitated his big brother.

''What's this about?'' Selena was looking from one to the other. ''Isn't this girl part of the landscaping crew?''

Ethan nodded. ''Sorry. I should have introduced you. Hannah, this is Selena Crain, my business partner. She flew here from Maine with some contracts.''

Hannah offered her hand, then seeing that it was dirty, lowered it to her side and said, ''Hello, Selena. It's nice meeting you.''

''Selena, this is Hannah Brennan. Hannah isn't just part of the crew. She owns the landscaping company.''

''How…interesting.'' The tone of Selena's voice was one of pure sarcasm. ''Won't it be nice when your business is successful enough that you can pay someone to take your place in the dirt?''

Hannah merely smiled. ''I hope that day never comes. I like playing in the dirt.'' She turned to

Ethan. "If your plans have changed, I'll understand."

He was already shaking his head. "Selena's just leaving. She has a four-o'clock flight back to Maine."

"All right. These are directions to my place." She handed Ethan a piece of paper with a map. "You can't miss it. It's the first big barn just outside of town." She stepped out the door, running her fingers through her matted hair. "You'd better give me an hour."

"That's all the time you need?" Ethan tucked the paper into his pocket.

"Yeah." She gave a short laugh. "That ought to give me time for a quick shower, followed by a long soak in the whirlpool."

"Sounds good to me."

At the smile on Ethan's face she felt her heart give a sudden bounce. Feeling completely flustered, she turned and nearly stumbled down the steps, calling over her shoulder, "I'll see you at six o'clock. Oh, and it was nice meeting you, Selena."

As she climbed into her truck and headed home, she wondered at the sudden burst of adrenaline. After the day she'd put in, she ought to feel exhausted. But the truth was, the thought of spending the evening with Ethan and his sons energized her. She thought he would want to cancel after seeing his business partner with him. She hadn't liked the feeling of dread that had started in the pit of her stomach. But she'd been wrong. That knowledge had her breathing long and deep.

She cranked up the air-conditioning as high as it would go and turned on her favorite oldies station to sing along with Paul McCartney's Wings about silly love songs. For some strange reason the words seemed to take on a whole new meaning.

"What was that all about?" Selena busied herself at the table, gathering up the signed documents and stuffing them into her briefcase.

"Hannah gave the boys a ride on her tractor this morning, and we're thanking her by taking her to a drive-in restaurant for dinner."

"A drive-in. Do they actually have such places anymore?"

Ethan laughed. "I'm about to find out."

Selena gave him a long, probing look. "This sounds suspiciously like a date."

"Don't be silly. I'm merely repaying a good deed."

"You seem awfully happy about this. Is this the same grief-stricken man who told me his life was over?"

Ethan's smile faded as he walked over to take the attaché case from her hand, then led the way to her car. "I did say that, didn't I?"

"That and a lot of other things. And if you recall, I was the one who told you that things would seem different if you'd give yourself some time." She opened the car door and turned to him, placing a hand on his arm. "Oh, Ethan. If only you'd listened to me. You didn't need to leave everything behind and start over in a new place. It wasn't a new place you needed. It was time."

"Maybe. But I've got to sort all this out in my own way, Selena."

"Away from the only home you've ever known?"

"If that's what it takes."

"And if the business suffers in the process?"

He settled her into the car and closed the door. Through the open window, he patted her hand. "I'm sorry to be putting you through all this. I know I've dumped a lot of stuff on you."

She closed a hand over his. "I'm a patient

woman. You and I have been through a lot since our college days. We'll weather this, too.''

"Yes, we will. Thanks, Selena." He stepped back. "Safe trip."

She turned the key in the ignition, then gave him a cool smile. "Next time we talk, you'll have to give me all the lovely details about the date at the…drive-in.''

Hannah heard the sound of a car and walked to the balcony to watch as Danny climbed from the back seat of his father's car. Ethan was busy unbuckling his younger son from his car seat.

"Hi." Hannah cupped her hands to her mouth and shouted, "I'll be right down."

By the time she'd hurried down the stairs, Ethan and his boys were standing beside the huge barn door, staring around with matching looks of curiosity.

"Wow." Danny's eyes were as big as saucers. "You live in a barn?''

"Yeah. Upstairs. I use this level for storage." She pointed to several tractors parked in a row, as well as her red convertible. One wall had been fitted with shelves from floor to ceiling, with a forklift to retrieve supplies. "Out there—" she pointed to an A-frame building that resembled an

Alpine chalet with gingerbread trim, where several college coeds were busy with customers buying flats of flowers ''—we handle retail to the public.''

''Pretty neat.'' Ethan looked around with a nod of appreciation.

''Want to see where I live?'' She led the way up the stairs, aware of the way Ethan followed close behind. Though she couldn't see his eyes, she sensed them focusing on her. It was a most unsettling feeling, and yet she couldn't deny the little thrill that raced along her spine.

Once upstairs she stood just inside the doorway while Ethan and the boys stepped inside and stared around.

''Wow. It's like a tree house, isn't it, Daddy?''

Ethan nodded, all the while staring at the woman who looked as fresh as one of her flowers in a denim miniskirt that displayed those long tanned legs to their best advantage.

Danny raced across the room and touched a hand to the twig headboard. ''Did you make this, Hannah?''

She shook her head. ''It was made by a man and his son who live in the woods a few miles from here. They make all kinds of twig furniture by hand. My sister, Courtney, sells some of it in her gift shop.''

The two little boys ran to the bathroom to gape at the painted ceiling and sunlight spilling through the skylights, while their father followed more slowly.

Ethan motioned toward the fairies overhead. ''Did you paint these?''

''My sister, Sidney. She's the artist I told you about.''

Ethan's voice was low with pleasure. ''This is great. Like some wonderful, mystical garden.''

''Thanks. I'll be sure to tell her.''

''She ought to paint you.'' He flicked a glance over her, pausing to admire her embroidered midriff blouse in some sort of gauzy white fabric that showed a tiny strip of tanned flesh. Without thinking he touched a hand to her arm. ''I don't know how you do it.''

At once she absorbed the sizzle that caught her by surprise. It took all her willpower to keep from stepping back. ''Do what?''

His eyes met hers, and the sizzle became a series of sparks that had her sweating. ''Look as cool and relaxed as though you'd done nothing more all day than be pampered in a spa.''

Was it possible for her bones to melt at a single touch? She found herself clutching the edge of the door for support. "Now you've seen my spa."

"Yeah." Though he hadn't meant to, he ran his hand along her arm, savoring the warm, firm flesh he'd been admiring from a distance. Up close she smelled of citrus. As cool and fresh as she looked. "And I've seen what you do all day. That's hardly my idea of nothing."

"Keeps me in shape."

"I'll say." His voice roughened. "I hope you don't mind the way I stare. It's hard not to." He drew her fractionally closer, loving the fact that she was tall enough that their eyes were nearly level. He leaned in, pressing his mouth to a tangle of curls at her temple. "You're the most fascinating woman I've ever—"

"Kitties!"

They turned at the sound of the excited squeals to see Danny and T.J. racing toward the balcony, where the two cats were dozing in the sunlight.

Danny skidded to a halt beside them and called to Hannah, "Will they bite?"

"Those two spoiled babies?" She wondered if her voice sounded as husky to Ethan as it did to her own ears. She'd been achingly aware of the fact that he was about to kiss her. What's more, she'd wanted him to. Desperately.

Now that she'd come to her senses, she was almost relieved at this distraction.

She moved away, putting distance between them. "The only things those two cats would ever consider biting are their wind-up toys."

While the two boys tentatively reached out their hands, the two cats arched their backs in pleasure.

Danny was smiling from ear to ear. "He's got a motor, Hannah."

"Quite a loud one, in fact." She laughed. "Those two like nothing better than someone who'll pet them."

"Do they have names?"

"They do. The gray-and-white one with the funny ear is Tiger. The other is Marmalade."

"Those are silly names."

"Not to Tiger and Marmalade. Just call them by name and you'll see what I mean."

The minute Danny called their names, the two cats got to their feet and began making figure eights between the two boys' feet.

"They think you have a treat for them." Hannah reached into a ceramic biscuit barrel and removed two cat treats, which she handed to the little boys. ''If you want to see two very happy kitties, just give them these.''

Danny and T.J. knelt down and offered each cat a treat, which they accepted from their hands. While the boys sat on the floor, running their hands over the soft fur, the two cats lay munching their treats and purring as loudly as motorboats.

Ethan remained where he was, unable to take his eyes off Hannah. Everything about her fascinated him. The look of her, slender as a willow and yet so strong. The sheer joy she seemed to take in the simplest of pleasures. A joy that radiated from her, touching everyone around her. It was impossible not to share that sense of happiness in her presence.

He'd come so close to tasting those lips. The thought of it had him sweating.

He crossed the room and stepped out onto the balcony, admiring the view. ''This is pretty amazing. Is it all yours?''

Hannah walked out to join him. ''Yeah. Mine and the bank's. As soon as my business started showing a profit, I paid back Poppie what he'd loaned me to get started and took out a mortgage to build the first greenhouse. Every time I pay off one debt, I seem to find something new that

I really need. Right now it's those blue spruces you see growing on that hill.''

He studied the even rows of hundreds of seedlings that dotted the hillside.

''They put me in debt for a hundred thousand. But if the weather cooperates, and I can keep them growing for enough years, I'll more than triple my investment.''

''Those are some pretty big ifs.''

Hannah laughed. ''Yeah. Especially the weather. A drought in their first year could stunt them.''

''Couldn't you install sprinklers?''

She shook her head. ''Not over so much distance. It just isn't cost-effective. So I pray for rain. But come winter, I'll pray for snow before the heavy-duty freeze sets in. Without the snow as insulation, a particularly hard winter kill could devastate them.''

''Sounds like quite a risk.''

''Oh, yeah.'' She laughed again. ''Poppie says my career choice is a bit like gambling. If everything lines up in my favor, I'll hit the jackpot. If not, I'll find myself in debt to my eyebrows. But at least I'm doing what I always dreamed of.''

''Then it's worth the gamble.''

Hannah nodded. ''Tell me what you do.''

"Design specialty software programs. If a company wants to send a rocket to the moon or build a better mousetrap, I design the software to make it happen."

"A computer geek?"

"That's what they call me."

She studied him with interest. "So that's why you asked me if I ever did my designs on a laptop? Have you already designed the software for landscape architects?"

"Not yet. But I'm thinking there may be a market for it. If I made it easier than carrying a clipboard, would you be interested?"

She shrugged. "Of course. But wouldn't you have to learn all about the subject before you could consider such a project?"

"Yeah." He gave her a heart-stopping grin. "Since I'm in the company of an expert, I figure I'll just hang around you and pick your brain." When she arched a brow he chuckled. "Don't worry. It'll be painless. Besides, I'm a quick study."

Her look was as much assessing as admiring. "You make it sound like a walk in the park. But I'm betting that brain of yours is already mulling over the possibilities."

His tone lowered. "You'd be amazed what this

brain of mine is mulling over at the moment, Hannah.''

Before she could respond he put a hand at her back. ''Come on. After the day you put in, I think it's time we fed you.''

When they were able to coax the boys to part with their furry new friends, they headed down the stairs to Ethan's car.

As he fastened T.J. into his car seat, Ethan glanced over to see Hannah helping Danny into his seat on the other side. When they were all settled in, Ethan turned the key in the ignition. ''Now where are these incredible hot dogs?''

''It's called the Dairy Devil. Take a right out of my driveway and follow the main highway until we're up in the hills.''

While Ethan followed her directions, Hannah turned to the two little boys, who were staring out the side windows with matching looks of eagerness.

Danny pointed to the rolling hills dotted with outbuildings. ''Are those yours, Hannah?''

''Most of them. My property ends right about… here.'' She nodded toward a low wooden fence lined with silver poplars that snaked across a flat stretch of land and disappeared over a ridge.

"Can you drive your tractor over all those hills?"

Hearing the wistful note in Danny's voice, she couldn't help laughing. "I could if I wanted. But I haven't had time to drive over all of it yet. Maybe when you and T.J. get a little bigger, you'll come and help me drive it. Would you like that?"

The two little boys clapped their hands and gave shrieks of excitement. "Oh boy, Daddy, can we help Hannah drive out here? Can we?"

Ethan shot her a sideways glance. "You realize they'll never let you forget that. One careless word and they'll hold you to it forever."

She couldn't help laughing. "I think it might be fun. I've always wanted to drive a tractor over my land. Who knows? Maybe when I reach the highest hill I'll just stand up on the seat and do my imitation of *Titanic*." She held her hands over her head and shouted, "I'm the king of the world."

"You can't be king," Danny corrected.

"Why can't I?"

"Because you're a girl. Isn't that right, Daddy?"

Ethan could hardly talk over the roar of laughter that welled up. "Oh, Hannah, you should see the look on your face." When he could find his voice he called, "I think, Danny, you may have just met the one woman in the world capable of being king if she wants to."

Hannah gave a playful slap at his arm. "You just said the right thing, Mr. Harrison. Anything else and you'd have found yourself lost and hungry, while I was busy hiking home. Alone."

Though the little boys in the back seat didn't understand the joke, they found themselves laughing along with their father and this woman who had given him back his sense of humor.

As they came up over a hill, Hannah pointed to the neon lights in the distance. "There's the Dairy Devil. Prepare to enjoy the best hot dogs and the thickest shakes in the world."

Chapter 8

"You were right, Hannah. This is the best." Danny patted his middle. "But my tummy can't take another bite."

"Ah, that's too bad, Danny." Hannah winked at him. "'Cause it's such a cute little tummy, and I was just about to bite it."

At her silly joke, both boys burst into laughter.

The four of them were outside the Dairy Devil, seated at a scarred picnic table.

Hannah seemed to be carefully studying the words and initials carved into the aged wood.

Danny asked, "What're you looking at, Hannah?"

"I'm looking for...this." She pointed. "I knew it would still be here." As the two little boys gathered on either side of her, she explained, "See that HB? That stands for me. Hannah Brennan. And the DF stands for Daryl Forestman. He drove me here the night he turned sixteen and got his driver's license."

The little boy glanced at his father. "Did he get in trouble for writing on the table?"

Hannah shook her head. "Everybody did it. In fact, the owner encouraged it. It was part of the teenage ritual here in Devil's Cove. Boys and girls would carve their initials in the wood and then everybody else would know they'd been here together."

"Why?" Danny ran his fingertip over and over the spot. As soon as he stopped, T.J. did the same.

"We were letting everyone know we were boyfriend and girlfriend."

Danny looked horrified. "Is he still your boyfriend?"

Hannah laughed. "He'd better not be. Daryl and his wife and three kids live in New York now. He's the producer of a daytime talk show on TV."

"Why didn't he marry you?"

"Because we were just friends, Danny. Daryl went away to college and we grew apart. It happens a lot, and people get on with their lives."

"If you were my girlfriend," the little boy said solemnly, "I'd never go away."

Hannah drew him close and pressed a kiss to his cheek. "That's just the sweetest thing, Danny. Thank you."

"Me, too," T.J. said, tugging on her sleeve.

With a laugh she drew him close and felt his chubby little arms circle her neck. "Yes. You, too. You're both my sweetest, dearest boyfriends. Now…" She caught her breath and took hold of both their hands. "Come on over here. I have something else to show you."

Ethan trailed behind, listening to the sound of her voice washing over him. Somehow, without even trying, she had completely mesmerized all of them with that boundless good humor.

"This place is called Dairy Devil because it's built right at the top of a hill known as Devil's Leap." Holding hands, she led the boys to a chained-off area of concrete, where a barrier had been built to keep curious people from getting too close to the edge. "From here you can look down and see the entire town. A couple of hundred years ago pirates used to come up here and watch for ships rounding the cape. Then they would race down the hill, swords between their teeth, and swim out to that sandbar, hoping the ship's captain wasn't aware of the danger of getting too close to it. Many a ship went aground there, and when that happened, the pirates would steal all the treasure in the ship's hold.''

Danny's eyes grew round. ''Did you know any of the pirates, Hannah?''

Her laughter rang on the air. ''Well, that was a little before my time. But I've read about them. And swimmers and divers still find broken bits of swords and remnants of ancient ships that the pirates looted.''

''Wow. A sword.'' The little boy turned to his father. ''Think we could find something like that, Daddy?''

Ethan shrugged. ''It's worth looking for. Maybe something will wash up on our beach one of these days.''

''Could we keep it?''

''I don't see why not.'' Ethan glanced at T.J., who was rubbing his eyes. ''But I think there's one little pirate ready to head for home. That is, unless you guys would like me to order another hot dog and chocolate shake.''

The two little boys shook their heads while Ethan and Hannah exchanged smiles.

"Come on, you two." Ethan picked up his youngest and caught Danny's hand. "Maybe you can teach Hannah the alphabet song on the way home."

"I can't believe how quickly they fell asleep." Hannah turned for another look at the two little boys, strapped firmly into their car seats. Their eyes were closed, their chests rising and falling in easy rhythm.

"It's the motion of the car. No matter how they try, they can't fight it."

"It's as though someone turned off a switch. One minute they were singing. The next they were out."

"That's how it is most nights. I'll be in the middle of their bedtime story and look around to realize they're gone."

"They're really sweet, Ethan. And you're so good with them."

"Thanks. So are you. I can't believe you don't have kids of your own. You're a natural."

She laughed. "Yeah. I've always been a sucker for kids and animals."

"It shows." He turned up the long curving

driveway toward the barn looming in the darkness.

He switched off the engine and stepped out, rounding the hood to open her door.

As she stepped out, he offered a hand and she accepted. Though she was aware of the heat of his touch, she was determined to keep things light.

"This was fun. Thanks for dinner."

"It's the least I can do to thank you."

"For what?"

"For making us laugh. I can't think of anything that touches my heart like the sound of Danny's and T.J.'s laughter."

"You make it sound like some rare, precious commodity."

"It is. Or at least it has been these past two years." He kept her hand in his. "Come on. I'll walk you to the door of your barn." That had him chuckling. "I don't believe I've ever said that to a woman before."

She drew back. "I'm not comfortable having you leave the boys alone in the car, Ethan. We'll say good night right here."

"All right." He looked down at their joined hands. And though he hadn't planned it, he drew her close and brushed his mouth over hers.

It was the merest touch of their lips. But the moment it happened, they were both forced to absorb the most amazing jolt, as though struck by a bolt of lightning that left them breathless and more than a little afraid.

"Ethan."

"Shhh." His hands closed over her upper arms, and he dragged her against him, his mouth on hers in a kiss so hot, so hungry, it nearly devoured her.

Against her lips he whispered, "I've been wanting to do that for such a long time now. I thought I knew how you'd taste, but I was wrong. So wrong. You taste even better than anything I could have imagined."

And then he was kissing her again, while his hands moved over her, drawing her even closer, until she could feel the thundering of his heart inside her own chest.

With a murmur of approval, her arms came around his neck and she gave herself up to the pleasure.

Some men, she thought, just knew how to kiss a woman. Ethan was such a man. His lips were firm, his mouth oh-so-insistent as it moved over hers, drawing out the sweetest sensations until she felt she was drowning in them. Her flesh was hot where he was touching her. And he was touching her everywhere. Her blood seemed to ebb and flow, starting a wild little pulse beating in her temples. And still she made no move to step away from the heat.

As he took the kiss deeper, she could feel her bones begin to go all fluid and soft, like wax to a flame. She had no will to stop him. If he chose, he could go on kissing her, holding her, forever. Or do with her what he pleased. She'd offer no objection.

Maybe it was the little sigh that escaped her lips or the way she opened to him, inviting him to take more. Whatever the reason, he suddenly seemed to go very still before lifting his head and stepping back.

The abruptness of his actions had her head spinning.

"Sorry." His voice sounded gruff.

"Why? I'm not sorry, Ethan. To be honest, I've been hoping you'd do this." She was smiling, but her smile faded when she caught his frown. The look in his eyes had her heart plummeting.

Now it was her turn to step back. "I can see that you don't share my...enthusiasm. My mistake."

Before she could turn away he swore and caught her arm, holding her still. "You're wrong, Hannah. I do share your enthusiasm. If it were up to me, I'd make wild, passionate love to you right here, right now, before you had a chance to change your mind. But that wouldn't be fair to you."

"I think I'll be the judge—"

He kissed her again, hard and quick, to silence her. Then with his hands at her shoulders holding her a little away, he sighed, "You've never once asked me about my wife."

"I assume you're divorced, that it wasn't very pleasant and that you'd get around to telling me when you were ready."

"You're right on only one count. It wasn't pleasant. But we weren't divorced. My wife is dead."

"Oh, Ethan. I'm sorry." At her little gasp he saw her eyes soften with sympathy. "You're feeling disloyal because..."

Before she could say more he stopped her. "The last thing I want to do tonight is speak of it. But before this goes any further between us, you deserve some cold, hard facts."

"All right. What are the facts?"

"My wife's life was ended by her own gun.

And though it was made to look like suicide, the authorities are divided on that. Some believe she was murdered.''

"Murdered? Oh, Ethan.'' The pain in his eyes had her reaching a hand to his cheek. "How horrible. For you and your sons. No wonder you don't want to speak of it.''

He caught her hand in his. The pain in his eyes fled, replaced by a look so hot, so fierce, it frightened her. "That isn't the end of it, Hannah.''

"What…?''

He shook his head, and the question died on her lips.

"To those authorities who believe Elizabeth was murdered, I'm the prime suspect. The only reason I haven't been charged is because there isn't enough evidence to arrest me, or anyone else.'' He looked down once more at their hands, and she thought she saw regret before he released her and stepped back. "If you'd be more comfortable having someone else finish the landscaping in my yard, I'll understand.''

He slid behind the wheel and closed the door before putting the car in Reverse.

As he backed away, he saw her illuminated in the glow of his headlights, standing as still as a statue. For one wild moment he thought about going back and telling her everything. It would feel so good to unburden himself to someone willing to listen. And he sensed that Hannah was the sort of woman who would listen and withhold judgment until the bitter end. But then the moment passed, and he knew that it was best if he went home. Alone.

On the long drive back, he berated himself for his damnable sense of honesty. For these few days he'd actually allowed himself to pretend that none of the horror of the past had been real. He'd almost begun to feel like every other young widower, playing with his sons, laughing, eating, sleeping and even allowing himself to consider a future.

It would have been fine except for one thing: there was too much goodness, too much honesty and integrity, in the woman he'd begun seeing in that future.

Whatever pain he felt, he had no right to inflict it on Hannah. Like his sons, she was an innocent party in this.

He'd been right to end it now, before it had a chance to flourish.

He swore softly and glanced at the two little boys who slept so peacefully. They would be heartbroken when Hannah stopped coming around. It seemed especially cruel to hurt them again when they'd been so wounded by all that had already happened in their young lives. But this was the right thing to do. Better to hurt them now than later, when the bond would have become deeper. He'd already sensed that they were opening their hearts to Hannah. And why not? She was the best thing that had happened to them in two years.

It had been fun to pretend for these past few days that he was just another guy, falling under the spell of a wonderful girl who could be part of a bright, shiny future. Now it was time for a reality check.

He lived under a cloud of suspicion, and would until the mystery of his wife's death had been solved. Until that time he had no right to drag someone as special as Hannah Brennan into his own particular kind of hell.

Chapter 9

Hannah stood just inside the doorway of the barn, watching as Ethan's car disappeared into the darkness. Without even realizing what she was doing, she climbed the stairs to her apartment. Once inside she moved mechanically across the room to the kitchen, where she turned on the kettle for tea. While she waited for the water to boil she stood on her balcony and lifted her head to stare at the midnight sky.

Ethan's admission had caught her by such surprise, she'd been absolutely speechless. That was a first for her.

After sensing his hunger and then his retreat,

she'd been mentally preparing herself to hear some sort of manly confession—that the torment of his wife's suffering through a long and painful illness had left him unable to love again. She'd even braced herself for a declaration that he had vowed never to marry for the sake of his wife's memory, or because he'd made a deathbed promise.

But murder?

When she realized the teakettle had been whistling for some time, Hannah shook her head, hoping to dispel her dark thoughts. As she returned to the kitchen and began to fill her cup, she paused and was forced to set the kettle down with a clatter. Murder wasn't something within the realm of her experience. It was simply beyond comprehension.

Ignoring the cup of tea, she began to pace. The authorities must have very compelling reasons for suspecting Ethan. Was it possible that this charming man, who painstakingly cared for his sons with no outside help, could have killed his wife?

As much as she wanted to deny such a thing, she had to admit that she had no idea what the face of a murderer looked like. Judging by what she'd seen in the media, seemingly ordinary men and women were capable of such horror.

But Ethan Harrison?

What did she really know about him, except that he was a stranger who had come to Devil's Cove without knowing a single person in town. He'd even relied on her mother, his real estate agent, to provide him with the basic necessities until he'd settled in. The beds he and his sons slept in had been chosen by someone else. The food in their cupboards had been left to chance.

Her sisters, without even knowing about him, had referred to Ethan as a mysterious stranger. Was that some sort of omen?

Desperately confused, she stopped her pacing and reached for the phone.

Hearing the familiar deep voice on the other end she took a shallow breath. "Poppie? I know it's late. Are you going to be up for a while?" She swallowed. "I really need to talk to you." After a moment she added, "Thanks. I'll be there in ten minutes."

"And that's all I know, Poppie."

Frank Brennan sat quietly, watching as Hannah, too agitated to sit, paced the room.

"One minute we're laughing over hot dogs

and shakes. The next he's warning me off by admitting that he is a suspect in his wife's murder.''

"Off." Her grandfather picked up on that single word.

Hannah stopped her pacing and turned to him. "What?"

"Off. You said he was warning you off. Off what?''

"Off…getting involved, I suppose." Hannah knew her cheeks were burning

"Are you? Getting involved?"

She swallowed. "Yeah. I guess we are." She hurried across the room and sat down beside her grandfather on the leather sofa in his old office. "At least I am, Poppie. And I think Ethan is, too. I'm pretty sure that's why he decided to open up about something so painful and hideous. He wants me to know what I'm getting into.''

"I see." The old man closed a gnarled hand over hers. "Then I guess we'd better find out all we can about the case.''

With a sigh he rose and walked to a wall of bookshelves, reading the labels until he removed a leather binder and carried it to his desk.

"Even though I'm retired, I still get the judicial journals. Let's see if there's anything about

a Harrison murder in Maine.'' He ran a finger
down the index. ''You say it was two years
ago?''

She nodded.

Finding what he was looking for, he began leaf-
ing through the journals until he suddenly muttered approvingly. ''Here we are.''

Hannah walked over to stand behind him as he
read aloud from the article. ''Elizabeth Harrison,
wife of millionaire Ethan Harrison, creator of a
line of custom software, was found dead of a
single gunshot wound in the garage of their home
in fashionable Fair Harbor, Maine. Because the
weapon belonged to the victim, authorities at first
believed the wound to have been self-inflicted.
But upon further investigation, the coroner determined that the path of the bullet seemed in-
consistent with that of a suicide, and though authorities are divided, some are calling it murder.
The case remains under investigation.''

''Can you find out more, Poppie?''

He looked up. ''I suppose I could make a few
phone calls. And there's always the newspaper
accounts, though I don't place much faith in
speculation. I much prefer cold, hard facts to idle
gossip and innuendo.''

''I don't care about gossip, either.'' Hannah

gave a long, deep sigh. "But I care about those two little boys and their father."

The old man pushed away from the desk and dropped an arm around his granddaughter's shoulders. "And I've always cared about whatever mattered to you, Hannah. Tell you what. Why don't you bring your young man and his sons to brunch tomorrow?"

Her look of surprise blossomed into a smile. "You wouldn't mind?"

"I'd like it. And I'm sure your grandmother would, too."

"Even though you may be entertaining a murderer?"

"Do you think he is?"

She shook her head solemnly.

"That's that, then." Frank cleared his throat. "Invite him."

"You'll remember to tell Trudy? I'd hate to catch her off guard."

"I'll tell her. Not that two small boys and one man should make a difference with the mountain of food she always prepares for our Sunday brunch." He chuckled. "But I'm sure of one thing. Your brother-in-law and I will welcome the extra men, for a change of pace."

Hannah wrapped her arms around his waist

and kissed his cheek. "Thank you, Poppie. I'm feeling better already."

"Good girl. Now see that you get some sleep. I'll look for you tomorrow."

He walked with Hannah to the front door, then stood waving as she drove away.

Instead of going upstairs to bed, Frank Brennan returned to his office, deep in thought. Finally he picked up the phone. What were old friends for, if they couldn't be called upon for a favor now and then?

Ethan stepped from the shower to the sound of Hannah's voice on his phone machine. Dripping water, he snatched it up. "Sorry. I had my head under water. What were you saying?"

Hannah's voice sounded breathy. "That's a relief. I was afraid you'd seen my name on your caller ID and decided to ignore me."

His tone deepened. "Don't ever think that, Hannah. If anything, I'm the one who's surprised. I didn't expect to hear from you again."

"You can't get rid of me that easily." She took a deep breath. "I'd like to take you and the boys to brunch at my grandparents' home."

"Why?"

"Because they invited you. Because I want

them to meet you and your sons. And because I'd like you to know my family.''

He thought he detected a slight tremor in her voice. ''You're sure you want to do this?''

''I'm sure.''

''What time?''

''Eleven. Their Sunday brunches always begin at eleven.''

''We'll be ready. Are you meeting us here?''

''If you don't mind.''

''Mind?'' He couldn't disguise his pleasure. ''I'd like that. And I know the boys will be thrilled.''

Hannah set down her phone and picked up the orange-and-white tabby, busy batting at the telephone cord with a paw.

As she carried the old cat across the room, she buried her face in its fur. ''Oh, Marmalade. I wish I knew what I was doing.''

She stood a moment on the balcony, watching the flight of a hawk. She told herself that she wanted her family to meet Ethan so that they could learn to care for him and his sons the way she did. But that wasn't entirely true. She was hoping, as well, that they would reinforce her belief that he was a good man who couldn't possibly harm those he loved.

What if, instead, she ended up bringing danger to their doorstep?

She pushed aside the sobering thought and deposited the cat on a cushioned chair on the balcony before hurrying inside to dress.

"Hannah's here, Daddy." With a shriek, Danny and T.J. slammed out the door and raced across the deck.

By the time the red convertible had come to a stop, the two little boys were standing side by side next to the driveway.

"Well." Hannah knelt down to accept their hugs before giving them both a nod of approval. "Looks like your dad laid out your Sunday best."

They wore navy shorts and crisp white polo shirts in a soft knit fabric. On their feet were new blue sneakers. Their blond hair was still wet from the shower. All they needed to look like perfect angels were halos of light over their heads.

As she took their hands in hers and started toward the deck, Ethan stepped out the door. She felt her heart do a lazy dip at the sight of him in pants and a silk T-shirt the color of caramel. Like his sons, his sandy hair was still damp.

The smile on his lips reached all the way to

his eyes, especially when he gave her a long, slow appraisal before turning to his sons. "Who is this woman? And what has she done with Hannah Brennan?"

Hannah couldn't help laughing as she glanced down at the ankle-skimming skirt and lacy shell in white silk. "I guess it would be a bit of a jolt to see me in lady clothes after my usual muddy jeans."

"More than a bit." He touched a hand to his heart. "If you're not careful, you may have to give me CPR."

"What's that?" Danny asked, looking from his father to Hannah.

"Commonly called mouth-to-mouth." Ethan continued staring at her in that way that always started her pulse racing.

As she walked up the steps he leaned close to whisper, "I was afraid I'd never see you again."

"So was I." She gave a little laugh. "You realize I'll have a lot of questions."

"Fair enough." He nodded. "I'll answer as many as I can."

"That's all I ask."

He looked at his watch. "Want to drive? Or do we have time to walk?"

"Let's walk." Hannah breathed in the fragrance of freshly turned earth and early-summer blooms that wafted across the yard on a gentle breeze. "We'd be foolish to waste a day like this."

With Danny and T.J. dancing along between them, they started down the driveway and past the gatehouse, where the uniformed guard waved.

Once they'd cleared the gated community, they walked along a sidewalk that curved past high fences abloom with roses that grew so lush and thick it was impossible to see the houses just beyond. When they started up the driveway of The Willows, Hannah saw Ethan studying the aged stone and brick facade, softened by ivy that had been neatly trimmed around doorways and windows. The lawn was carefully manicured, the gardens showing the years of love and hard work that had been lavished upon them.

Hannah's eyes danced with unconcealed humor. "Welcome to our humble abode."

Chapter 10

They followed the sound of voices to the back-
yard where the rest of the family had already
gathered on the patio. It was a sight that always
had Hannah smiling. Her grandfather stood at the
brick barbecue, wielding giant tongs that he'd
fashioned from several discarded garden imple-
ments to turn an assortment of meats and fish on
the grill. Sidney was arranging flowers in a crystal vase, while Courtney was setting the table
with a fashionable mix of family heirlooms and
one-of-a-kind pieces she'd bought from local artisans. Emily and Jason stood to one side, hands
linked, faces bent close, wearing the secret smiles

of newlyweds. Trudy was wheeling a trolley laden with covered dishes from the kitchen. And in the midst of all the commotion, Hannah's grandmother, Bert, sat on a glider, watching her family with a look of pure contentment.

"Well." Frank's chore was forgotten as he caught sight of Hannah and her guests. Hurrying over he bent to kiss her cheek. "Now our family is complete. I was beginning to worry that you'd overslept."

"Not a chance, Poppie. But the day is so perfect, we decided to walk." She laid a hand on Ethan's arm. "Ethan, this is my grandfather, Judge Frank Brennan. Poppie, this is Ethan Harrison."

"Sir." Ethan extended his hand and was surprised by the strength of the old man's grip.

"Welcome to The Willows, son." Frank turned to the two little boys. "Such handsome lads."

"This is Danny and this is T.J." Hannah dropped an arm around each of their shoulders.

"Danny, is it? You're the picture of your father." The old man bent down and offered his hand. "Tell me what T.J. stands for."

"Thaddeus Joseph." Danny answered for his little brother.

"A fine name. Can you say it yet, lad?"

T.J. nodded. "Taddus Josep."

While the others smiled, Frank said, "Good for you, lad. By the time you're able to say it comfortably, that nickname will have stuck. You'll be T.J. for a lifetime. I speak from some authority. I was Frankie from the time I was born. By the time I'd ascended the bench, I wanted to be called Francis Xavier, because I thought it sounded judicial and proper. But it was too late. All my friends called me Frankie, and do to this day. Those who don't—" the old man winked at the little boy "—call me Poppie. I ask you, what kind of respect can I get with a name like that?"

The two boys were grinning as the rest of the family gathered around.

Hannah's mother greeted Ethan warmly. "Are you still in love with the house?"

"Yes, thanks to you. You made my move effortless." He paused a beat before saying, "Your daughter tells me that everyone calls you Charley."

"That's my name." She winked at Danny and T.J. "If you think Frankie is a tough name for a judge, just think about a woman my age still being called Charley."

"A woman your age?" Frank lifted his daughter-in-law's hand to his mouth for a gallant kiss. "To me you will always be twenty-five and my son's gorgeous bride."

She blushed like a schoolgirl. "Which is why you're my favorite father-in-law."

As the others gathered closer, Hannah handled the introductions. "These are my sisters. Sidney."

Ethan accepted her handshake. "The artist."

"I see Hannah's been discussing her family."

"And why not, when she has such beautiful sisters."

Hannah turned to her youngest sister. "This is Courtney."

"I've seen your gift shop in town, though I haven't had time to stop in yet."

"Come on by. You'll find some really unusual things for that new home of yours."

Ethan nodded. "I will."

"And this is Emily."

"The doctor." He glanced toward his two sons. "I'll be calling to arrange a well visit soon."

"I look forward to it."

"And this is Emily's husband, Jason Cooper."

Ethan arched a brow. "The author?"

Jason nodded as he offered a handshake.

"You write fantastic books. Your latest, *Secrets in a Small Town,* was fabulous."

Jason brushed a kiss over his sister-in-law's cheek. "I see you finally found a guy with good taste."

That had everyone laughing.

Ethan studied Jason. "I thought you lived in Malibu."

"I did." Jason dropped an arm around his wife's shoulders. "But Emily's medical practice is here, and I figured I can write anywhere. We've decided that Devil's Cove is to be our home from now on."

Ethan watched as Hannah's grandmother approached. Despite the cap of white curls, her eyes held the same twinkling light that he'd always seen in Hannah's.

"Ethan, my grandmother, Bert Brennan."

As they shook hands Ethan said, "I don't think I'd be comfortable calling you Bert."

"Try Mrs. B.," Jason offered. "It's what her students have always called her."

"You teach?"

"I did." Bert gave him a warm smile. "I finally retired this past year."

As Hannah and her sisters exchanged knowing

looks, Hannah explained. "If you can call it retirement. I think Bert tutors more students now than she did when she was on the school's payroll."

"And why not?" Trudy Carpenter ambled up. "Not only does Mrs. B. offer her services free, but she also sees to it that the kids put away a mountain of cookies and a gallon of lemonade before she sends them home."

Hannah lay a hand over Trudy's. "If that's true, then you're Bert's coconspirator. You know you like baking for all those teenagers."

"That's because you and your sisters have decided that cookies are fattening. I have to find someone who appreciates my baking."

Hannah turned. "Trudy, this is Ethan Harrison and his sons, Danny and T.J. This is our housekeeper, Trudy Carpenter. She's been keeping us all in line for as long as I can remember."

The housekeeper, who was as round as she was tall, gave Ethan a long, direct look. "If you're a friend of Hannah's, you're welcome here." She turned her attention to his sons. "I hope you two like homemade cookies."

Danny seemed surprised. "You really bake them. In an oven?"

"I really bake them. In an oven. None of those store-bought cookies in this house."

"Can you make chocolate chip?"

"They're my specialty."

Danny's eyes grew even bigger. "They're my very favorite." He turned to his little brother, who was nodding his head. "And T.J.'s, too."

"That's good." She pointed to the trolley. "There's lemonade over there. And after brunch, I'll have a tray of cookies hot from the oven."

The two little boys looked questioningly at their father. When he gave a nod of approval, they followed Trudy across the patio and were twitching with excitement as she poured them frosty glasses of freshly squeezed lemonade.

Watching, Ethan couldn't help chuckling. "Those two have never tasted cookies from the oven."

"Then they're in for a very special treat." Frank rubbed his stomach. "Nobody bakes chocolate chip cookies like Trudy. Nobody."

"And Poppie should know." Hannah and her sisters shared a laugh.

"Careful," Emily warned. "If your sons have a sweet tooth like Poppie's, they're about to become Trudy's slaves for life."

"Why don't we all sit." Bert tucked her arm

through Frank's and led the way toward the table, with the others following.

When they were settled around the big patio table, Bert sat at one end, the judge at the other.

Hannah indicated a chair beside her grand father's. "Why don't you sit here, Ethan, and we'll put the boys between us."

As Trudy began removing the lids from silver trays and passing them around the table, she paused beside Danny and T.J. "I hope you two like waffles."

Danny nodded. "Daddy makes them in the toaster sometimes."

The housekeeper wrinkled her nose to show her disapproval. "Not those kind of waffles. These are made in a waffle iron, and topped with real Michigan maple syrup and black walnuts, freshly whipped cream and strawberries picked this morning from the judge's garden."

Ethan took his first bite and closed his eyes on a sigh of pure pleasure. When he opened them, he looked over the heads of his two sons to see Hannah grinning.

He shook his head. "This is amazing. I'm not sure my boys can appreciate this yet, but I don't believe I've ever tasted food this good."

Trudy gave a sigh of pleasure before walking away.

As the housekeeper crossed the patio to retrieve something from the kitchen, Hannah looked around the table. "Well, we weren't too far off base with the name of Trudy's next slave. But who knew it would be the father instead of the sons?"

"Do you come from a big family, Ethan?" With the meal finished, Bert and Ethan were seated on a glider, watching as Frank showed off his strawberry patch to Danny and T.J. on the far side of the yard.

Ethan shook his head. "My parents died in a plane crash when I was just about Danny's age. I don't even remember them, except for the things I've been told. I was raised by an aunt and uncle, my father's older brother. Their own kids were already in college by that time, so I was treated more like a grandson than a son."

"How fortunate that you had some relatives to open their home to you."

He nodded. "I must have been a handful to those two quiet, bookish people. I started boarding school when I was ten."

"So young."

He shrugged. "I didn't mind. It gave me the chance to be with other boys my age. I remember playing a lot of soccer and football. And it was there that I discovered computers. I fell wildly, madly in love with all the possibilities that opened up with my first computer. By the time I'd finished college, I'd already designed half a dozen software programs and was offered top jobs with all the big computer software companies."

"Which one did you go with?"

He smiled. "I started my own, with a friend from college. My uncle was horrified when he learned that I was planning to use my inheritance for the start-up costs. Though he tried his best to sound encouraging." His tone softened. "I've always been glad that he lived long enough to see my business flourish."

"How long ago did he pass away?"

"It's four years now."

"And your aunt?"

He looked away. "She cut me out of her life two years ago. There's been no contact since."

Bert laid a hand on his arm. "I'm sorry, Ethan. I know that your wife died under mysterious circumstances. I should think that would be enough to bear, without the censure of those you love, as well.''

At his arched brow she said softly, ''I don't believe Hannah was betraying your confidence by speaking openly to her grandfather.''

''Of course not.'' He paused before adding, ''I'm just surprised that you would welcome me to your home after hearing such a thing.''

''It is apparent that you and your boys matter to Hannah. And Hannah matters to us.''

He gazed out over the expanse of water at the base of their yard. ''The case is still open and I'm still a prime suspect. What if I should be accused and brought to trial?''

''Are you guilty of your wife's death, Ethan?''

The blunt question had him turning to look at her directly. ''No. I loved Elizabeth. But knowing I'm innocent isn't enough. I have no right to drag anyone else into this slime.''

''Hannah?'' Bert smiled. ''In case you haven't noticed, my granddaughter isn't the type to be dragged into anything. If there's any dragging to be done, it will be Hannah doing it.''

Ethan looked across the yard to the object of their discussion, kneeling in the grass between his boys. Though he wasn't aware of it, a look of softness came into his eyes. Even his voice softened. "You know her very well."

"I do indeed." For long moments Bert studied him as he watched her granddaughter. There was no denying what she could see in his eyes.

When at last she spoke, her voice was little more than a whisper. "If Hannah chooses to stand with you, Ethan, she will have the love and support of her family. And if the day comes that you are called upon to prove your innocence, you may be assured that the Brennans will be there to stand beside her."

Ethan shook his head. "I've never known a family like yours, Mrs. B. You're a formidable force to be reckoned with. You'd make terrifying foes."

She smiled then, a smile that was so much like Hannah's it dazzled him. "We would indeed. Keep that in mind, young man. When you see Hannah working like a man, you may be tempted to forget that she has the tender heart of a woman. But if you should ever break that heart, you would answer to all of us."

Chapter 11

"Look, Daddy." Danny and T.J. came rushing up to their father, holding out little tin buckets filled with strawberries. "Hannah's Poppie let us pick all we wanted."

"Judging from those red stains on your mouths, I'd say you ate as many as you put in the buckets."

"Just a few. Hannah said they wouldn't give us tummy aches."

"Maybe not. But added to the plate of chocolate chip cookies you put away and the gallon of milk and lemonade, I think we're going to have to do some serious walking to work off all that food.''

''But Courtney said we worked hard on her sailboat.''

''That looked like fun.'' And had caused Ethan a moment of panic when he'd watched his two sons leaving on the little boat with Hannah's sisters. It had been quite a jolt to his heart to give up control of his sons' safety into the hands of someone else. He'd been the sole caregiver for so long now, it was hard to let go for even a few hours. But Hannah had assured him that both her sisters were excellent sailors and that his sons were in capable hands.

''It was fun. Courtney made us wear life jackets. And she let us steer.''

''Steer,'' T.J. echoed. His chubby little hands made steering motions in the air.

Danny nodded. ''And the sails puffed up and made us feel like we were flying. And when we got to Sidney's place, she took us to her studio and let us paint.'' He held up a wrinkled sheet of paper. ''Look. I made a sailboat. And T.J. made a garden.''

''Garden.'' T.J. held up his drawing for his father's approval.

"That's great. Were you drawing Hannah's garden?"

When the little boy grinned, Ethan ruffled his hair. "You two have had quite a day."

The little boys nodded.

"But like all good things, it's time for this day to end."

"Do we have to go?" Danny's smile faded, and beside him, T.J. pouted while rubbing at his eyes.

"Yes, we do."

As they bade goodbye to Hannah's family, Trudy came shuffling across the patio carrying a pretty little box tied with blue ribbons and handed it to Ethan.

"What's this?"

"A few treats for tomorrow."

"Oh, boy." Danny was grinning from ear to ear. "Are they—" he held a hand over his mouth to whisper loudly "—chocolate chip cookies?"

Trudy winked. "Warm from the oven."

Ethan moaned. "How am I ever going to get them to eat store-bought cookies after this?"

"Did you just say that nasty word, 'store-bought'?"

While the others roared with laughter at the

look on Trudy's face, Ethan said goodbye to his hosts.

Hannah kissed her grandparents. "Bye, Bert. Poppie. Thanks for a wonderful day."

Danny was skipping ahead when he suddenly turned back and, imitating Hannah, said, "Bye, Bert. Bye, Poppie. This was the best day of my whole life."

As they rounded the corner of the house, Ethan looked slightly embarrassed. "I hope your family wasn't offended by that."

Hannah reached up to touch a hand to his cheek in an achingly sweet gesture. "Obviously, you weren't looking at my grandparents' faces. If you were, you'd have seen that they were positively beaming. And quite frankly, so am I. I think all little boys should have a Bert and Poppie in their lives."

Ethan smiled into her eyes. "I can't argue with that."

"Hey, little guy." Ethan paused along the sidewalk when he realized that Danny was lagging behind. "Getting tired?"

Danny nodded.

"Okay. Come here. I'll carry you on my

back.'' He crouched down, and the little boy wrapped his arms around his father's neck.

They caught up to Hannah, who was cradling T.J. in her arms, his face nestled against her shoulder. His eyes were firmly closed, his breathing slow and easy.

''My boys have had quite a day. So has their dad.'' Ethan lifted his face, inhaling the perfume of the night. ''Smell that air.'' It was sweet with the fragrance of peony and rose, of lilac and lily. It reminded him of Hannah.

He glanced over at her. ''Do you ever get tired of flowers?''

''Never.'' She laughed. ''Would you?''

''I never used to think about it. Now I figure I'll never get enough, thanks to you.''

When they reached the gatehouse, they waved to the guard. Once inside the grounds they could hear the gentle lap of water on shore and were greeted by the automated trouble lights that had been installed, switching on the minute they drew near the house.

''Here we are, little guy. Home.'' Ethan climbed the steps and deposited his son on the deck.

Too weary to stand, Danny crumpled and sat on the doorstep with his back to the closed door.

Seeing him, Hannah smiled gently. "I think someone needs to be carried up to his bed."

"He can walk." Ethan turned to her with arms outstretched. "I'll take T.J. He has to be heavy."

She shook her head. "I can manage. Why don't you carry Danny, and I'll take T.J. upstairs?"

"If you don't mind." Ethan picked up his older son and led the way inside, turning on lights as he made his way to the stairs.

Once in the boys' room, Hannah lay T.J. down on his bed and began removing his sneakers before slipping him gently under the covers. The little boy never stirred.

Danny sat on the edge of his bed and rubbed his eyes. "Do I have to brush my teeth?"

Ethan chuckled. "Not tonight, son. I think if you tried, you'd fall asleep at the sink."

Ethan covered him with a blanket and bent to kiss his cheek. "Good night, Danny."

"'Night, Daddy." The little boy looked at Hannah standing beside his father. "I had the best time. I haven't decided what I liked most— sailing Courtney's boat, painting in Sidney's studio or picking strawberries with Poppie." He yawned loudly and closed his eyes. "I wish I could spend every day with your family, Hannah. They're the best.''

She sat on the edge of the bed and brushed a kiss over his cheek. ''You know what they say about wishes, Danny. Maybe if you wish hard enough, they'll come true.''

Ethan felt a hard, quick tug on his heart as she stood and crossed the room. When he held the door she brushed past him and he felt his body strain toward hers. With a last look at his sleeping boys, he snapped off the light and closed the door before following her down the stairs.

As they stepped into the kitchen he was frowning. ''I think Danny said it best, Hannah. This has been a terrific day. You have an amazing family. Thank you for sharing them with us.''

''You're welcome.'' She turned at the door and, seeing the frown line between his brows, lifted a finger to the spot. ''If it was such a great day, why this?''

He stepped back, avoiding her touch. She was the reason for the frown, though he'd never admit that. ''I guess I was just thinking about all the things I should have done today instead of playing.''

''I see.'' Stung, she turned away. ''Well, I won't keep you from them any longer.''

"Hannah, I didn't mean…" As she opened the door he placed a hand on her arm. Just a touch, but he felt the heat jolt through his body like a flash of lightning. At once he lowered his hand to his side and clenched it into a fist, determined not to touch her again. He needed, for both their sakes, to be strong enough to resist temptation. "It's not that I'm ungrateful. I couldn't help but see the way my two little boys were lapping up all that love that your family seems to share with such a generous spirit. I'll never forget it. But…"

"But now you'd like me to leave." She nodded. "I understand. Good night, Ethan."

Without warning she leaned close and brushed her mouth over his. It was the merest whisper of a kiss, but she heard his quick intake of breath before he dragged her close and savaged her mouth with a kiss so hot, so hungry, she was nearly devoured by it.

Hannah gave no thought to resisting. The suddenness of it seemed to electrify her, and on a moan of pleasure she wrapped her arms around his neck, adding to the heat that flowed between them.

Ethan was already regretting his moment of weakness. This wasn't at all the way he'd planned it. And now, unless he found the strength to end this as quickly as it had begun, they were both going to take a fall.

Calling on all his willpower, he wrapped his fingers around her upper arms and held her at arm's length while he fought for breath.

Then before he could lose his nerve, he released her and took a step back.

For long moments Hannah stood perfectly still, struggling to suck air into her lungs.

When she looked at him, she saw his eyes narrowed on her with such intensity she actually shivered.

"Sorry." She tried to smile, but her lips trembled.

Seeing it, he cursed and called himself every sort of fool. But still he held his silence.

"That was bold of me, Ethan. But then, I've never been a shrinking violet."

When he didn't offer any response, she turned away and stepped through the doorway.

"Good night, Hannah." He stayed where he was, desperate to hold on just a minute more. Once she was in her car, he would allow himself to relax.

He listened to the sound of her footsteps receding. Closing the door, he leaned against it and took several deep breaths before crossing to the stairs.

The last thing he wanted was to go to his room. The silence of it mocked him. As did the sight of the big bed. Empty. Always empty. The very word was a knife to his heart. Empty like his life. Like his future.

Instead of climbing the stairs, he walked to the window and studied the moonlight slanting golden ribbons across the waves. For the longest time he stood there, feeling more miserable than he could ever recall.

He'd thought the loss of Elizabeth was the lowest point of his life. But seeing Hannah today with her family, hearing all the jokes and laughter, seeing the easy way they were with each other, made him realize just what he'd missed. And was missing still.

His fault. He had no one to blame but himself. She'd made it very plain, with that one kiss, that she was willing. But how could he lead her on when he had nothing to offer her? She had her whole life ahead of her. What sort of future could he ever hope to have if he didn't clear his name?

Only a coward would ever drag a woman like Hannah into a mess like this.

He didn't know how long he'd been standing

there. Minutes or hours. But he suddenly became aware of a shadow moving on the deck.

Striding across the room he tore open the door. And then he simply stared.

"Hannah."

"I just realized something."

"What?"

"How fine and noble you're trying to be."

She smiled. A smile that seemed to hide a hundred secrets. The light spilling over her cast her in a golden halo. Everything about her seemed to shimmer and shine. Her eyes staring into his with a heat that was like a laser straight to his heart. Her hair, golden in the moonlight. Her tanned arms reaching out to him.

"I don't know what you're—"

The words died on his lips when she stepped through the doorway and touched a finger to his mouth. She kept her eyes steady on his.

"Who appointed you my keeper, Ethan? Was it Poppie? Or did you come up with this all by yourself?"

"I don't have to answer that."

She gave a deep-throated laugh. "I'll get it out of you. I'll either kiss you until you're breathless, or we'll arm wrestle and I'll shame you into telling."

He couldn't hold on to his frown. "Do I get a choice?"

"Sure. The same choice you gave me." She stepped closer so that their bodies were touching.

She saw his eyes narrow. "You have the most expressive eyes, Ethan. Did you know they give away all your secrets?"

"What are you? A witch?"

"Of course. All women are. Now I'm going to read your mind." She touched a fingertip to his temple and gave him a little cat smile. "You didn't really want to send me home, did you?"

His voice was a low growl. "Whether I did or not, if you've got a brain in that head, you'll get out of here right now."

Her chin jutted like a prizefighter's. "Make me."

He wanted to shake her. Without thinking, he caught her by the shoulders and realized, too late, that he'd made a terrible mistake. Now that he was touching her he had to hold her. His arms came around her, dragging her close. But now that he was holding her, it was even worse. He had to kiss her.

Against her mouth he whispered fiercely, "I tried to warn you, Hannah."

"Yes, you did." She lifted her hands to frame

his face. "And it was so noble and manly of you. But I happen to have a mind of my own." She paused just a beat before adding, "Don't worry. I won't hate you in the morning, Ethan."

There was a flash of humor before his eyes narrowed on hers and he claimed her mouth in a kiss so desperate, it sealed both their fates.

Chapter 12

He'd never known a mouth so clever. He would have gladly feasted on it for hours if it weren't for the wild rush of needs that had him driving her back against the wall, his hands fisted in her hair.

He might have worried that he was too rough, except that she had already wrapped herself around him and was driving him slowly mad.

She ran hot, wet kisses over his face, then returned again and again to his mouth, as though she couldn't get enough. And her hands. Those strong fingers that could steer a heavy tractor or roll out a length of sod were now clawing at his back, nearly shredding his shirt as she yanked it over his head.

She sighed at the sight of his naked chest, laying her palms flat against his hair-roughened flesh, taking a moment to breathe. But only a moment. Then her greedy mouth began nibbling a trail of fire across his chest, and he wondered that his heart didn't simply explode.

"Wait." He tore away her ankle-skimming skirt, leaving it to pool at their feet. Then he tugged the white silk tank over her head, and for the space of a heartbeat his throat went dry at the sight of that lithe, perfect body covered only in wisps of nude lace.

"Hannah," he said softly. He pressed his forehead to hers, struggling to calm his raging passion.

Maybe it was that quiet whisper that had her going so still. Until this moment she'd been so sure of herself. Sure enough that even his attempt at rejection hadn't had the desired effect. Instead of running home to weep or sulk, she'd stayed and fought for what she wanted. And the minute she'd been assured that she'd been right, she had been overcome by a frenzy of need for this man.

But now, seeing that hunger in his eyes, hearing the fierceness of his tone, she felt an icy trickle of fear. Fear of what they were about to share. Because she knew in her heart that this wasn't a mere whim. This was, on her part, the real thing. This was what she'd been waiting a lifetime to find. And she wanted desperately for it to be equally important to Ethan.

"Losing your nerve?"

She lifted her chin. "Of course not."

"You're not a good liar, Hannah." The smile curved his lips. Warmed his voice.

"I'm not afraid." But her breath hitched as he lowered his mouth to the lace that covered her breast.

"You should be."

Heat poured between them, and she wondered that she didn't burn to ash. She could feel her legs trembling, and clutched frantically at his waist to keep from falling as he slowly drove her higher and higher toward the edge of madness.

On a shuddering breath she managed to whisper, "Are you afraid, Ethan?"

"Terrified." He kept his eyes on hers as he unsnapped her bra and tossed it aside before feasting. He felt her flinch as his fingers encountered the elastic of her lace bikini before dipping inside.

''Ethan.'' Hovering on a high, sheer cliff, she could do nothing more than hold on.

''Shhh.'' He covered her mouth in a savage kiss as he took her on a wild ride to the first peak of pleasure.

She was wonderful to watch. Those honey eyes widened, before glazing over as she reached the crest. Her hands tightened at his waist, then seemed to go limp.

She was mad to touch him as he was touching her. In a frantic burst of energy she tore at the fasteners at his waist until the last of his clothes joined hers on the floor. Her hands moved over him, and she smiled at his low moan of pleasure that sounded more animal than human.

He'd wanted to go slow. To touch and taste and savor to his heart's content. But now, with her hands on him, the need was so sharp, so intense, there was no stopping the avalanche that was bearing down on them both.

With his hands pressed to the wall on either side of her head, he leaned into her and kissed her until she was breathless. The feel of all that warm, naked flesh imprinting itself on his was the sweetest torture. He knew he could no longer deny the hunger that was aching to be fed.

When she wrapped her arms around his neck,

he lifted her and started toward the sofa across the room. Halfway there he paused to kiss her again. That was his undoing. The rush of heat, the tide of need, swept over him with such force, he was staggered by it.

They dropped to their knees on the floor, locked in a fierce embrace. The most incredible heat rose up between them, clogging their throats, leaving their skin slick with sheen. Their breathing was shallow and ragged.

"I can't wait another minute." On a sigh he dragged her down, with only a rug to cushion her from the hard floor, before covering her body with his. "I need you, Hannah. I need..." Those were the only words he could manage before fusing his mouth to hers.

Her body arched. Her hips rose up to meet him as he entered her. With a long deep sigh that seemed to come from her very soul, she took him in and began to move with him, to climb with him.

The world could have ended in that instant, and neither of them would have noticed. There was only this time, this place, the intense pleasure they shared.

"Oh, Ethan." Her eyes were fixed on his, and

she locked her arms around his neck as she felt herself reaching the crest.

Hearing his name on her lips was the sweetest sound he'd ever known. It was the last thing he heard before he took her with him over the edge.

"You okay?" With his face buried against her throat, the words were muffled.

"Ummm." It was all she could manage as she waited for her world to settle.

"Sorry. I was rough."

"No." She lifted a hand to his cheek. "You were…amazing."

That had him lifting his head to study her eyes. His grin was quick. "Thanks. I'm a little out of practice. You were pretty amazing yourself." He rolled to one side and gathered her close. "Must be all those hours of digging in the dirt and laying sod."

She couldn't help laughing. "Yeah. That makes a girl nimble."

"You are that." He ran his hand along her back, up her side, encountering the soft swell of her breast, and felt her trembling response. It thrilled him to know that even now, spent from lovemaking, she wasn't immune to his touch.

"Sorry about the hard floor." He glanced toward the overstuffed sofa across the room. "I was aiming for that."

"Great aim, William Tell. Remind me to never volunteer if you want to display your skill at shooting an apple off someone's head."

Ethan threw back his head and roared. "Oh, Hannah. You're exactly what I've needed."

"That's me. The comic relief."

He leaned up on one elbow and took her hand, lacing his fingers with hers. "I love your sense of humor. But more, I love your goodness. When I see you with my boys, I start to believe that the past can be put to rest and we can have a future."

She looked at their linked fingers, then up at him. "Believe it, Ethan."

He stared down into her eyes. "I didn't want you involved in this. I want you to know that I did my best to discourage you."

"I noticed."

He shook his head. "I thought I'd handled it well enough. What made you decide to come back for more?"

"I saw the look in your eyes. It was more eloquent than any of the words you spoke. I was in my car and ready to head home to sulk when I remembered Poppie's words of wisdom, spoken since I was just a girl. 'Nothing ventured, nothing gained.'"

"You? Sulk?" He shook his head. "I don't buy that. Your grandmother warned me that you have a mind of your own." The smile was back on his lips. "She never mentioned your fabulous body, though. I guess she figured I'd have to discover that on my own." He leaned down to brush his mouth over hers.

The heat was back. This time instead of a rush, it stole over them softly, warming their flesh, their blood, as they came together.

He managed to pry his mouth free for a moment. "Want to try for the sofa?"

She wrapped her arms around his neck and drew his head close to nuzzle his lips. "Maybe later. For now, I'll settle for this. Just this."

And then there was no need for words as they lost themselves in each other.

"I'm still finding it hard to wrap my mind around the woman I see rooting around in the dirt in my yard as the girl who grew up in that lovely old mansion."

Ethan and Hannah lay snuggled together on the sofa. The only light in the room was the moonlight spilling through the skylights over-

head. There had been little time to sleep while
they explored the wonders of their newly discovered love.

Ethan studied the way she looked, eyes heavy-
lidded, lips thoroughly kissed. His fingers played
through the strands of her hair.

Hannah smiled. "I guess there are some who
expect the Brennan women to be pampered dar-
lings. It's just never been my style."

He brushed a kiss over her mouth. "Baby, I
like your style. I like it as much as I like your
family."

"They are special, aren't they?"

He nodded. "I was a little apprehensive about
taking the boys there, but five minutes into our
visit, I felt as comfortable as though I'd known
all of them for a lifetime."

"That's always been their special gift. Whenever my sisters and I brought friends home, Bert
and Poppie would treat them like family. And
Trudy always had little treats for them to take
home."

"You don't know what that means to Danny
and T.J. The worst part about what's happened
in the past two years is that loss of family."

Because he'd told her about his own childhood, Hannah touched a hand to his. "It has to

be twice as hard for you, having lost what little family you had.''

''I really believe, if I'm ever able to clear my name, that my aunt will come around in time.''

''I hope so, for her sake as well as yours. Doesn't she realize that she has two adorable great-nephews that she doesn't even know?''

He nodded. ''But it's her pride that's keeping her away. She believes I've dragged the family name through the mud.''

''But not by choice. Can't she see that she's only adding to your pain?''

Ethan gave her one of those heart-stopping looks. ''My fierce little champion. Do you know how much it means to me to have you on my side?''

She snuggled closer and wrapped her arms around his waist. ''Why don't you tell me?'' As he started to speak, she stopped him with a long, lazy kiss. Against his mouth she whispered, ''Better yet, why don't you show me?''

''Hannah Brennan.'' His words were spoken on a moan as he dragged her close. ''I do like the way you think.''

''Umm. Is that coffee I smell?'' Hannah pushed hair from her eyes as Ethan settled himself beside her on the edge of the sofa.

"It is." He handed her a steaming cup.

"Oh, this is heavenly." She sipped, then glanced at the tray. "What's all that?"

"Sustenance. You've been exerting way too much energy all night. I'd hate to have you slow down now. So I scrambled some eggs."

"My hero." She stood up and tied an afghan around her like a sarong, before tucking into the food.

"This is good." She glanced around. "Where's yours?"

"I thought we'd share."

"Oh." She pretended to snatch the plate away before handing it to him.

He arched a brow. "You sure you can spare this?"

"Only a bite or two. Then I'd like it back."

He took a taste, then fed her another bite. "Have I told you how much I enjoy watching you eat?"

"How much?"

"Almost as much as I enjoy watching you work. You're amazing."

"While we're passing out compliments, I'll admit that I love the way you take care of your two sons. It can't be easy doing it alone."

He shook his head and reached for the coffee. But she saw the sadness that came into his eyes.

Setting down the plate, she put a hand over his. "Would it help to talk about Elizabeth?"

He kept his face averted. "We met in college. It's funny, but we seemed to have nothing in common. I was a jock, in love with computers. She was a dancer who spent all her spare time teaching an inner-city dance class. But we had one common thread. We were both lonely, young and in love, and desperately wanted to be part of a family. We married right after graduation. Shortly after Danny was born, we started talking about having another baby. But that was the same time that Elizabeth started feeling threatened."

"About what?"

He shrugged. "At first it was just this vague feeling that little things were happening that weren't quite right. One night Elizabeth got sick after drinking some juice. Later, when she tried to find the container, it was missing. Another time she swore she heard someone beside the bed in our room. But when she woke me and turned on the light, we were alone."

Ethan stood and began to pace. "By the time T.J. was born, Elizabeth was convinced that someone was out to hurt her. I have to admit, I really didn't take her fears as seriously as I should have. But at her insistence I had an alarm system installed and helped her pick out a hand-gun.''

''A handgun? With two little boys in the house?''

He nodded and ran a hand through his hair. ''She had a locked drawer up high enough that neither of them could reach it. I thought with all that protection, that would be the end of it.''

Though she wanted to go to him, Hannah remained where she was. ''Tell me the rest, Ethan.''

''I was at work when the police arrived. It was a cold October day, just two weeks after T.J.'s birth. A neighbor had spotted Danny out in the driveway in his bare feet. She knew Elizabeth well enough to know she would never allow that. The neighbor suspected that Elizabeth may have fallen asleep with the new baby, so she started phoning. When she got no answer, she called the police. They found T.J. asleep in his crib. Elizabeth was in the garage, in a pool of blood.

''At first they suspected suicide. It happens sometimes if a new mother is suffering from postpartum depression. I assured them that Elizabeth had been just fine, except for those vague fears about her safety. There'd been no hint of depression. If anything, she'd been so vital and filled with a love of life. After the autopsy, the coroner couldn't confirm or deny that the gunshot had been self-inflicted.

"That changed everything. Though I'd been at work the entire time, there were times when I'd been alone, with no witnesses to verify that I was actually there. To this day, the authorities consider me a prime suspect in my wife's death, simply because they can't prove my guilt and I can't prove my innocence." His voice lowered with conviction. "But I know this. Elizabeth didn't take her own life. She simply couldn't."

"How could the police allow you to move clear across the country?"

"They couldn't stop me. But they let me know that I'm still under suspicion." He shook his head. "Nobody wants this solved more than I, Hannah. I left, not to run away, but because I needed to know that my sons were safe from not only the one who killed their mother, but also to find release from the unrelenting notoriety. Ours was a small town. Everywhere we went, Danny and T.J. were the objects of pitying looks. That's no way to live. But I haven't given up on finding Elizabeth's killer. I hired a team of private investigators and told them to spare no expense to unearth the truth, no matter where it leads.''

''What makes you think they can do what the police can't?''

He turned, and she could see the darkness in his eyes. ''I'm convinced that the authorities, believing me to be the killer, have missed important evidence.'' His tone lowered to a fierce whisper. ''They're saying that if it was murder, it was the perfect crime. I'm not buying it. No one is capable of committing the perfect crime. If it takes me a lifetime, I swear I'll prove them wrong.''

Hannah did go to him then. Wrapping her arms around his waist she lifted her face to his. ''If it takes you a lifetime, I hope you'll let me be part of it.''

He framed her face with his hands and stared down into her eyes. What he saw there had his heart soaring. ''Oh, Hannah. What did I ever do to deserve you?''

''You came to the right town at the right time, and hired the best woman to decorate your yard and your life. Now kiss me quick.''

He lowered his mouth to hers and tried to show her, with long, deep kisses and soft, quiet sighs, just how much she meant to him.

Chapter 13

"Where are you going?" Still half asleep, Ethan reached out and caught Hannah's wrist as she eased away from the sofa.

"Home."

"Now?" His eyes snapped open. "It's barely dawn."

"Yeah." She leaned close to brush a kiss over his lips. "I've got a business to run. Time to get ready for another week of sodbusting."

"I thought that was for ranchers in the Old West."

"Maybe. It's also what landscapers do to earn a living."

"Don't go. Give it all up. Stay here with me and be a kept woman."

Hannah laughed. "Now that's a tempting offer. Let me give that some thought." She tapped a finger on her crossed arm. "Okay. I've thought it over and my decision is—" she eased the silk tank over her head and stepped into the wrinkled skirt "—no. Sorry. I like my work. It may not be quite as satisfying as what we shared all night, but it's a living."

He scrambled to his feet and drew her close. "At least you could leave me with a goodbye kiss."

"Uh-uh." She gave him a knowing look. "One kiss will lead to another, and next thing you know we'll be right back on that sofa."

"I didn't hear you complaining an hour ago."

"No complaints." She touched a finger to his mouth. "There's nothing I'd like better than to stay and be lazy all day. But one of us needs to be practical."

He rolled his eyes. "Now I find out you're not only beautiful, sexy and fun to be with, but practical, too."

"Every rose comes with thorns, Mr. Harrison." She turned away and snatched up her keys. As she started toward the door he walked up behind her and drew her back against the length of him.

Nibbling her ear, he muttered, ''Will you have dinner with us when you're finished with your work?''

''That depends. What're you planning to feed me?''

''All the protein and carbs I can cook.''

''Mmm.'' She sighed as he nibbled his way down her neck. ''I guess I could be persuaded.''

''I've seen how hard you work.'' He turned her into his arms and rained kisses over her upturned face. ''I mean to restore all that spent energy as fast as possible, and maybe even persuade you to stay the night again.''

''If you promise to kiss me like this, I'll consider it.'' She stepped back more than a little reluctantly. ''Now I really have to go.''

Ethan walked with her as far as the deck and watched as she climbed into the little red convertible and waved goodbye.

He was humming a little tune as he walked inside and headed up the stairs to the shower. Minutes later, as he stepped out and reached for a towel, he heard the sound of Selena's voice on his message machine. Ignoring the puddle of water, he snatched up the phone while glancing at the clock. "Isn't it a bit early for a business call?"

There was the slightest pause before Selena said, "You're there. I thought maybe you'd gone somewhere for the weekend."

"What makes you think that?"

"Because I phoned you yesterday afternoon and left an urgent message, and you didn't even bother to respond." She gave an exaggerated sigh. "Apparently it's true what they say. Out of sight, out of mind. Now that you've physically left the business, it's all too apparent that you've left it emotionally, as well."

"I'm sorry, Selena." Ethan glanced down at the flashing red light on his message machine. "I forgot to check my messages. What was so urgent that you're calling at dawn?"

"The Davis contract hit another snag. They wouldn't agree to the delivery date we'd promised them. I needed to be certain you could live up to an earlier date, but when I didn't hear from you, I had to make an executive decision without your input. I hope you're in the mood to work day and night, because you're now going to have to deliver the new software program for their approval by the end of the month."

He ran his fingers through his hair, swearing

silently. Aloud he merely said, "If that's the agreement, I guess I'll have to live with it."

"You could always come back to Maine, and we could work on the program together."

"Not a chance." He balanced the phone between his ear and shoulder while he fastened the towel around his waist.

"That sounds ominous. Don't tell me you're considering making this move to Nowheresville permanent."

When he didn't respond, she changed the subject. "You never reported back on that little date to the drive-in. Was it a trip back in time to the sixties? Did they have teenage girls carrying trays to your car? Or maybe that landscaper, what's-her-name, did the fetching for you."

"Her name is Hannah. And the boys and I had a great time. In fact, Selena, we're having the time of our lives here in Nowheresville. And every day we're here it's starting to feel more and more like home."

The silence on the other end of the line seemed to go on for several beats before Selena finally said, "I can see I caught you at a bad time. You'd better go make yourself some coffee. Call me back after the caffeine kicks in."

Ethan replaced the receiver and caught sight of

his frown in the mirror. After flying through a night of pure fantasy, all it took to bring him to earth with a thud was a well-aimed dart tipped with reality.

Ethan and the boys stepped out onto the deck and watched as Hannah and her crew began stowing the equipment for the night. The retaining wall was completed, with lush plantings of fernlike foliage and flowering shrubs flowing over and around the boulders, softening every inch of space.

Hannah approached, hair damp and sweaty, jeans and T-shirt streaked with dirt. She tipped up her water bottle, draining it. "Well? What do you think?"

"It's beautiful." Ethan touched a hand to her cheek. "Almost as beautiful as you."

She winked at his sons and pressed her palm to his forehead. "Either your daddy is feeling feverish, or his eyes have gone bad. That retaining wall is beautiful. All I am is filthy and sweaty."

Danny giggled. "Daddy's right, Hannah. You're beautiful."

She dropped down on one knee and touched his forehead, then did the same with T.J. "It's just as I thought. All the Harrison men seem to have acquired a rare strain of Devil's Cove roseola spectacle psychosis. The dreaded rose-colored glasses syndrome. I'd call my sister, Dr. Emily, to see if there was a cure, but I'm not sure that's wise.''

"Why?" Danny asked in perfect innocence.

"Because then you'd see me as I really am, this filthy, sweaty creature, and would no longer see me as a dazzling beauty. I think I prefer your vision to the truth.''

The little boys knew by the way their father was laughing that Hannah was making a joke. And though they didn't quite understand, they laughed along with him, enjoying the moment.

"Daddy says you're staying for dinner.''

"First I'm going home to soak in my tub.''

"Why don't you take a bath here?''

"Because I also need to get clean clothes.''

"Then will you come back here to eat?''

"Absolutely.'' She waved to her departing crew before turning toward her truck. "Give me an hour.''

"Can we go along?" Danny shouted. "We could play with Tiger and Marmalade while you take your shower.''

Even while Ethan was protesting, she paused,

then returned to the deck. "Now why didn't I think of that?" She glanced at Ethan. "If your father has no objections, I'd like to take you both along."

"In your truck?" Danny was already clapping his hands.

T.J., looking suddenly pleased, did the same.

"Why not? There's room for both of you."

When she turned to Ethan, he merely shrugged. "If you're sure…"

"I am." She caught the boys' hands. "Come on. Let's get your car seats out of your daddy's car. Tiger and Marmalade have been lonesome for playmates."

With Ethan's help, she buckled the two boys into her truck before sliding behind the wheel.

"Think you can stand being alone for an hour?" she called through the open window.

"I'll try not to go stir crazy." He waved until her truck was out of sight.

As he turned toward the house, it occurred to Ethan that Hannah's question hadn't been too far off the mark. Since Elizabeth's death the boys had rarely been out of his sight. Their safety was his primary concern. But maybe, he thought with a trace of unease, it wasn't the only reason for his vigilance. Two busy little boys assured him that he would have little time left over for himself. And so he had welcomed the distraction, knowing it kept him from dwelling on the pain of his loss.

"We made it." Hannah and the boys breezed onto the deck while she tapped her watch. "With five minutes to spare."

"Marmalade let me hold him," Danny was shouting.

"Me, too." T.J. was twitching with excitement.

Hannah inhaled the fragrance of onions and peppers on the grill. "Oh, something smells wonderful."

Ethan turned from the grill, then nearly dropped the tongs in his hand at the sight of her. "You've done it again. Turned Hannah the landscaper into a fairy princess. Are you some sort of magician?"

She arched a brow. "Oh. You mean this old thing?" With a laugh she twirled like a model, causing the hem of her cool mint-green summer dress to swirl around her strappy little sandals. The dress was backless, displaying an expanse of tanned flesh that had him drooling.

With Danny and T.J. watching, Ethan crossed

the space separating them and drew her close for a quick kiss on her cheek.

"Daddy's kissing Hannah." At Danny's chant, T.J. laughed and clapped his hands.

Surprised and more than a little pleased at their reaction, Ethan looked over at his sons and wiggled his brows. "Do you think I ought to do it again?"

"Yes. Yes." With the two little boys shouting and dancing around them, Ethan brushed a second kiss over her cheek before stepping back.

Hannah laughingly brushed at her cheek to hide the rush of heat she'd been forced to absorb. Just being close to Ethan caused her pulse rate to soar. "Kisses are very nice, Mr. Harrison. But I believe you promised me protein."

"And I always keep my promises." He turned away and picked up a fluted glass.

She studied it as he handed it to her. "Champagne? What's the occasion?"

He merely gave her one of his most charming smiles. "It goes with protein."

"Ah." She sipped and watched as he began filling a platter.

"Hannah, sit here," Danny called.

She took her place between the two boys and clinked her glass to their glasses of milk.

With giggles, the boys drank their milk and watched as their father filled their plates. Hannah reached over and began cutting T.J.'s meat and vegetables into small bites.

She glanced at the platter that Ethan was holding out to her. "Is that steak? Thick and marbled with fat and dripping blood?"

"I hope that's the way you like it."

"Oh, be still my heart." She stabbed a steak and set it on her plate.

"I made some pasta to go with it." Ethan set a bowl of pasta loaded with tomato sauce and baked cheese beside her plate and watched as she helped herself to a mound of it.

Danny glanced over. "Are you going to eat all that, Hannah?"

"You bet. And probably more if your daddy doesn't take it away from me."

Across the table, Ethan's smile lit his eyes as he sipped his champagne and watched Hannah tuck into her meal. He loved watching her eat. In fact, he loved watching her do everything. Work. Talk. Laugh with his sons. He'd never known anyone like her. And as much as he enjoyed seeing her with his boys, he could hardly wait until later, when Danny and T.J. were asleep, and he could have her all to himself.

"Hannah gave me a string and told me to shake it in front of Marmalade. Daddy, that old cat started jumping and leaping and…"

The little boy's voice trailed off as a car rolled to a stop in the driveway. When the door opened, Selena lifted out an attaché case and headed toward them.

"Selena." Ethan got to his feet and stood at the top step of the deck. "What are you doing here?"

"More trouble with the Davis account." When she saw Hannah, something flickered in her eyes. But when she spoke, her voice was smooth as silk. "I see I'm disrupting your meal. Sorry. But that's business."

"I tried phoning you several times, only to get your answering machine. I had no idea you were flying all this way again. Why didn't you just work out the problems over the phone or on e-mail?"

"Because I prefer face-to-face."

"I see. Well then, join us." Ethan took the briefcase from her hand and offered her his chair. "I'll put this inside and get another plate."

"Don't bother. I ate on the plane."

"A glass of champagne, then?"

She arched a brow. "I never turn down a glass of champagne. What vintage?"

"Would you like to check the label?"

She shrugged. "Never mind. It doesn't matter."

Ethan walked inside.

While he was gone, Selena glanced at Hannah, addressing her for the first time. "Is this part of your landscaping contract? Dinner with the boss?"

"Actually, this is a bonus." Hannah touched a napkin to her mouth and pushed aside her half-eaten meal. "Danny and T.J., did you say hello to Selena?"

"Hello, Selena," the boys said in unison.

"Still no nanny, I see. Which is why your daddy is too distracted to attend to business. He should have listened to me and considered a good boarding school."

Hannah sucked in a breath. "You're aware, I suppose, that Ethan attended boarding school at an early age?"

"I see he's sharing his personal history with you." Her tone sharpened. "Boarding school didn't hurt Ethan, and it wouldn't hurt his sons. Right now he's too confused to sort things out. But in time he'll come to his senses and realize that he needs to focus on the details of the business—which he and I built at great financial risk—or we could both end up losing a fortune.''

''So this is about you?''

At Hannah's quiet question, Selena rounded on her. Before she could speak, Ethan stepped out and handed her a crystal flute before topping off Hannah's drink. As he did, she looked up at him and they shared a smile.

Seeing it, Selena set down her glass with a clatter, causing them to look over.

''Sorry. I guess I'm just weary from so much travel.'' She managed a smile. ''I hope you have a spare room. I think I'd like to sleep now, and then we can get started ironing out the difficulties with the Davis contract in the morning.''

''You're staying the night?'' Ethan was shaking his head. ''Sorry. Of course you are. You couldn't possibly fly out to Maine at this time of night.'' He thought a moment. ''There are several spare rooms, but they're not furnished.''

''No matter. I can sleep on the sofa.''

Hannah turned to Ethan. ''There's a lovely old inn in town. The Harbor House.''

''It sounds…quaint.'' Selena chuckled. ''But I'm not going to stay in some roadside motel. I'll be just fine on Ethan's sofa.''

"Nonsense." Ethan started toward the door. "Do you happen to know the number of the Harbor House, Hannah?"

"Sure. We've been going there since we were kids." She picked up her glass and followed him inside.

Minutes later, she returned to find Danny and T.J. eating in silence while Selena stood at the railing, tapping a foot and sipping her champagne.

"Good news," Hannah called. "Ethan was able to reserve their best suite for you."

Selena turned slowly and seemed about to say something when Ethan stepped out the door carrying her attaché case.

His smile was as broad as Hannah's. "You heard?"

Selena nodded.

"Turn left when you leave the gatehouse and follow the main street into town. You can't miss the Harbor House."

"I'm sure I won't have any trouble finding it." Selena's glance stayed fixed on Ethan, ignoring Hannah and the boys. "Thank you for going to all this trouble, Ethan. I'll see you in the morning."

Chapter 14

"Thank heaven for the Harbor House." Ethan pressed his mouth to a tangle of hair at Hannah's temple.

The two, pleasantly sated, lay in a tangle of arms and legs on the sofa. The only light came from the moonlight that streamed through the skylights overhead.

"You don't mind that I suggested it?" Hannah turned toward him, her fingers playing with the hair on his chest.

"Mind?" Ethan chuckled. "It was brilliant. I was beginning to feel trapped. I was trying to figure out just how I could lock Selena in an empty room upstairs so she'd be out of our way.''

''You realize she's in love with you.''

At Hannah's words he froze.

Seeing his reaction she sat up, unmindful of her nakedness. ''Don't tell me you didn't know that?''

He shook his head, as though to clear it. ''I'm not denying it. It's become painfully obvious. But I wasn't aware of it until Elizabeth pointed it out. In fact, her words were stronger than yours. She told me that Selena was obsessed with me.''

''Obsessions can be dangerous, Ethan.''

He nodded, deep in thought. ''I know what you're thinking. But the private detectives I hired went over Selena's file, looking for any flaw in her alibi, and gave her a clean bill of health. They did the same with every other person who might have come in contact with Elizabeth on the day of her death.''

Hannah sighed. ''The perfect crime.''

Ethan ran his hands through his hair before pulling on a pair of camp shorts and walking to the kitchen. A short time later he returned with two steaming cups of tea. After handing one to Hannah, he sat down beside her.

She touched a hand to his. "Tell me about Selena."

He sipped, then looked away. "We met in college. She's brilliant. Dean's list. A string of degrees. Daughter of a prominent Boston family. An only child, expected to earn her M.B.A. and take over the reins of the family business. Instead, after finding out that I wanted to design specialized software programs for businesses, she offered to invest her money and come in as an equal partner."

"Does she pull her weight?"

"Absolutely." He nodded. "She's a workaholic. Can get by on a couple of hours sleep a night. Never suffers jet lag, no matter how many time zones she flies through. Our first year in business she lined up so many clients, it became impossible to keep up with the demand. She's the one who is always nagging me to work harder, faster, longer hours. If it weren't for Selena, I doubt our business would be as successful as it's become."

"Did she seem upset when you got married?"

He shrugged. "Yes, but only insofar as she considered it a distraction. She's so focused on her work, she thinks I should be the same and allow nothing to interfere."

Hannah thought a moment before saying softly, "Earlier this evening Selena referred to Danny and T.J. as distractions."

He winced. "Yeah. She's made it plain that she thinks I spend way too much time being a father. She gently suggested boarding school for my sons, but I've made it just as plain that it's not an option. I've been down that road."

Seeing Hannah's look of disapproval at the mention of boarding school, he smiled. "In Selena's defense, I have to say one more thing, which to me is more important than anything else. When all my friends deserted me after Elizabeth's death, Selena stood by me." He set aside his cup. "For that alone I'll be indebted to her for the rest of my life."

Hannah sipped her tea. "Friends that loyal are hard to find." She brightened. "I guess I'd better make a greater effort to like her, even though she's made it obvious that she isn't fond of me."

Ethan smiled before taking the cup from her hands and placing it on the end table with his.

When she arched a brow he drew her close and brushed his mouth over hers. "Her loss." Feeling her trembling response, he took the kiss deeper. Against her mouth he whispered, "Because I happen to be very fond of you, Hannah Brennan, and I'm about to show you just how much.''

''Don't tell me it's morning already.'' Ethan reached out for Hannah, only to find her already dressed and perched beside him on the edge of the sofa.

''All right. I won't tell you. But I'm leaving.'' She bent down and pressed a kiss to his lips before heading for the door.

''Dinner tonight?''

She paused. ''Are you coo ng?''

''Of course.''

She nodded. ''I'll be he . Now I've got to run.''

As she drove home, H nah thought about what Ethan had told her. F r his sake, she would crank up the charm whenever she was with Selena Crain. If the woman was a friend of Ethan's, Hannah would do what she could to make her a friend, as well. She hadn't met anyone she couldn't win over when she put her mind to it.

''We'll be putting the playscape here.'' Hannah unrolled the plans she'd drawn up with Ethan's approval, and her crew gathered around for their assignments.

Martin Cross had already directed several of the crew to spray the vegetation. In the heat of the day, it had quickly begun to wither and die, making it easier to remove. Now the crew began digging up the old sod and replacing it with mulch that would soften the ground if the boys should fall from the swings and slide. Still other workers were busy putting together the equipment to be installed as soon as the area was prepared.

Hannah waved to Danny and T.J., who were watching from the safety of the deck. Through the wall of windows she could see Ethan and Selena bent over documents spread out on the kitchen table. Selena's car had been there when Hannah and her crew had arrived for work.

Hannah couldn't help smiling, wondering if Ethan had found time to shower and dress and straighten the sofa before Selena's arrival. No matter, she thought. If he wasn't bothered by having their romance made public, why should she? Sooner or later Selena would have to accept the fact that her business partner was getting on with his life.

Getting on with his life. The phrase had Hannah humming a little tune. Until Ethan and those two adorable boys, she'd wondered if she would ever find someone with whom she would care to share her life. Not that she hadn't been perfectly content with the way things were going. But now that these three had come along, she was deliriously happy. There was nothing more she wanted or needed.

Was this how Emily felt when Jason had come back to Devil's Cove? Hannah thought of the pure bliss she saw in their eyes whenever her sister and brother-in-law looked at each other. Would they be able to tell, just by looking at her, that she was feeling the same sort of wondrous joy?

"That's okay, Kevin." Hannah cupped her hands to her mouth and shouted, "I'll get those things out of the way." Seeing the young football player heading her way on the tractor loaded with sod and earth, she snatched up an armload of shovels and hauled them to a waiting truck.

She spotted her water bottle lying on the ground and wondered how it had landed there when she'd left it beside her truck. She snatched that up, as well. When the tractor was safely past, she looked around with approval.

"You know what?" She grinned at her crew. "We're a darned good team."

She lifted her water bottle in a salute before

tipping it to her mouth. She was aware of the noxious odor of weed killer at the same instant that she felt her mouth start to burn like the fire of hell.

Though a tiny trickle of liquid slid down her throat, leaving it raw and blistered, she managed to spit most of it out before grabbing Martin Cross by the front of his shirt.

Her eyes were red and watery. Her words were little more than a strangled whisper. "Get me to Emily's clinic right away."

She was only vaguely aware of his strong arms wrapping around her, hustling her toward his truck while he shouted orders at the stunned crew. As he turned the key in the ignition, she leaned her head back, forcing herself to breathe in great gulps of fresh air. Every breath burned her mouth and throat and lungs. But she was determined to clear her head and remain coherent until she could get the help she needed.

"I won't have a definitive answer until the lab has concluded all the tests." Emily took Hannah's hands in hers and squeezed. "But from the smell, I haven't a doubt that the water was laced with weed killer. Now we need to know why.

Have you ever used separate containers for mixing this stuff?''

Hannah shook her head, grateful that she'd had the presence of mind to cling to her water bottle. ''Never. It's been a firm rule from the beginning. All our containers are clearly labeled. In a business like mine, there are too many accidents just waiting to happen. I don't leave any room for my workers to mistake one solution for another.''

''Then my next question is, how can you be certain the water bottle you drank out of was yours?''

''My name is clearly marked on the side.'' She held it out to her sister. ''With so many crew members, it's a necessity.''

''So, if this was a deliberate act, anyone who wanted to lace your water with that weed killer wouldn't have any problem knowing which bottle was yours?''

Hannah sighed. ''I know where this is headed, Emily. You want to know if any of my employees might be holding a grudge.''

''I'm not the only one who'll want to know.'' Her sister wrapped an arm around her shoulders. ''I called Boyd Thompson. He's coming by your place later to get a complete report.''

Hannah nodded. Boyd was the police chief of Devil's Cove. "I understand."

"Now go home, Hannah. The burning should be gone in a few hours. I want you to take this sedative as soon as Boyd leaves, and try to sleep. I've already alerted the family. Bert and Poppie are going to be spending the night at your place." Emily touched her forehead to her sister's. "Thank heavens you didn't swallow more than a drop."

"Yeah. I'm just glad that stuff smells so nasty. Otherwise…"

She saw her sister give an involuntary shudder and knew without asking what her fate might have been.

When she stepped out of the clinic, Martin Cross was waiting. "Your sister told me to drive you home. And I'm going to stay there until Boyd Thompson and your grandparents get there."

"Thanks, Martin." She settled herself inside and closed her eyes. "What about my truck?"

"I'll have one of the guys bring it to your place later."

As he drove, she dialed her cell phone and waited for Ethan's familiar voice.

"Hannah. What are you doing on the phone? Why didn't you just knock on the door?"

She heard the smile in his voice and was warmed by it. "I'm not in your yard, Ethan. I'm in Martin's truck, heading home. I won't be returning to work until tomorrow."

"What about dinner?"

"Sorry. I'm afraid I've lost my…taste for food."

"You?" He laughed. "Now that's hard to believe. What's going on, Hannah?"

"There's been an…incident." She tried to keep the drama from her voice as she told him what had happened. His tone went from warm to frigid in the blink of an eye.

"Dear God. I've been so busy I didn't even realize you were gone. I should have been there with you."

"Don't be silly. There was no time to tell you what had happened. I'm just leaving my sister's clinic, and she's already given me something for pain and something to help me sleep."

"I hate to think of you alone out there. I could come by later with the boys. Just to make sure you're all right."

"Don't worry, Ethan. The police chief is coming by to make his report."

"The police chief?"

"Yes. And Emily has already enlisted the aid of my entire family. Bert and Poppie will be spending the night. I'll see you in the morning."

There was a long pause, and when he spoke his voice was little more than a whisper. "I wish I could be the one spending the night with you."

"So do I." Hearing a voice in the background, she paused. "Is Selena still there?"

"Yeah. She said she'll need at least one more day to finalize the contracts. But she wants you to know that you were right. She loves her accommodations at the Harbor House."

"I'm glad." She closed her eyes and fought a wave of exhaustion. The painkiller had muddled her brain. "Good night, Ethan. Kiss Danny and T.J. for me."

"I will."

"And one for you." She knew that Martin could overhear everything, but somehow it didn't seem to matter anymore. She didn't care if the entire town knew that she was involved with Ethan Harrison.

Involved. Her fingers closed around her cell phone. The word didn't do justice to the things she felt for Ethan. She loved him. Desperately.

And loved those two dear little boys just as much.

There. She took a deep breath. That hadn't hurt a bit. She had always been more comfortable with the truth than with dancing around it. She was as involved as a woman in love could be. And she was equally certain that the object of her affection shared those feelings.

Despite Martin's truck jostling over bumps and ruts, she fell asleep with a smile on her lips before they were halfway to her place.

Chapter 15

"Anything else you can think of, Hannah?" Police Chief Boyd Thompson looked up after making notes in his report.

Boyd was a big, beefy man who had come by his love of law enforcement naturally. His father had been police chief of Devil's Cove when Hannah was a little girl. Boyd had looked up to his father, and now took the badge and the responsibility that came with wearing it, seriously.

Hannah struggled to stay focused. The painkiller seemed to have numbed her brain as well as her body. With Bert seated on one side of her and Poppie on the other, both watching her with quiet concern, she felt as she had when she'd been ten and had taken a tumble from a friend's horse. On her father's orders, a different family member had been assigned to wake her every hour to be certain she hadn't suffered a concussion. But her grandparents had forsaken a night's sleep to stay with her around the clock.

This was far more important than a tumble from a horse.

"It's hard to think, Boyd. But I haven't fired any employees, and I can't think of any former employees who carry a grudge."

"Somebody went to a lot of trouble, Hannah. Now the intention might have been to kill you, or it might have been meant as a warning." He gave her a steady look. "The Devil's Cove grapevine is alive and well. And word around town is that you're involved with a man who's a prime suspect in his wife's death."

She gave him an indignant look. "Ethan didn't do this."

"So you say." Boyd's gaze locked on hers. "My homicide files are filled with the names of women who trusted some good-looking guy with murder on his mind."

Hannah looked down to find her grandfather's hand covering hers. Her own was cold. So cold.

She closed her other hand on his, grateful for his support.

"It wasn't Ethan." She said the words with quiet conviction. "I know that sounds foolish to a man of the law. But I know in my heart it wasn't him."

"All right. Give me the name of anybody, no matter how impossible it might seem to you, who doesn't like you." He held up a hand when he saw her open her mouth to protest. "I know this is a small town and you don't want to get anyone in trouble. I can promise you I'll be discreet. I'm not interested in idle gossip, now, or a simple misunderstanding. This had the potential to turn deadly. I want the names of anybody who has given you bad vibes lately." Again that steady look as he said, "Come on, Hannah. Help me out here."

His words, spoken in that stern, commanding voice, had the desired effect. As long as she was being truthful, she needed to face one more fact. Whether the intention had been to bring her serious harm or simply to frighten her, anyone who would do such a thing was dangerous. Though Ethan had defended Selena as a loyal friend, the most obvious suspect in Hannah's mind was the woman in Ethan's home. In Ethan's business. In

Ethan's life. The woman his own wife had considered obsessed.

It hit Hannah with such force, she moaned aloud before saying softly, "There is one person. I hope I'm wrong." She turned to her grandfather, and her eyes filled. "Oh, Poppie, I hope I'm wrong because she means a great deal to Ethan."

"Give me a name, Hannah." Boyd's voice brought her attention back to him.

She met his eyes. "Ethan Harrison's business partner, Selena Crain."

Hannah's dreams were dark and vivid. A sleek jungle cat with feral eyes sat on a branch over her head, watching as she approached on horseback. Just as she passed beneath, the cat sprang, sending her horse into a frenzy, rearing and bucking while she clung frantically to the saddle. Once she was thrown to the ground, she was helpless to evade those lethal claws and deadly teeth.

She awoke with a start and lay very still. When her heartbeat gradually returned to normal, she became aware of subdued voices on the balcony. She sat up and was delighted to see Ethan sipping tea and talking quietly with her grandparents.

"Ethan?"

At the sound of her voice he turned and walked to the bed. "I'm sorry. I know you need your sleep." He was staring at her with such hunger, she felt her heart actually leap in her chest. "But I couldn't stay away."

"I'm glad you came. I really needed to see you."

"But now I woke you, Hannah."

"No. I had a dream."

"Not a very good one from the looks of it."

She nodded.

He sat on the edge of her bed and touched a hand to her cheek. "I'm something of an expert on bad dreams."

She caught his hand and pressed a kiss to the palm. "I know. And I'm sorry you've had to go through so much pain. My dream is gone and forgotten now that you're here."

"Maybe this will make it go away for good." He handed her a small, beribboned box. "The boys and I bought this at your sister's gift shop."

Hannah looked up at him. "She never mentioned it."

"I swore her to secrecy." He smiled. "I've been saving it for a special time to give it to you."

When Hannah merely stared at it he said, "Go ahead. Open it."

Hannah lifted the lid and found, nestled in tissue, a whimsical enameled lapel pin of a beautiful angel watering some pansies.

"The moment we saw it, we all thought of you. Danny calls it his garden angel. He thought it was the one he prayed to at night. I didn't have the heart to tell him that was a guardian angel. Anyway, he said it reminds him of you. So you're now his garden angel."

"Thank you." Hannah closed her hand around the pin. "I love it."

"I'm glad. The boys have been nagging me to give it to you."

Hannah glanced toward the balcony, expecting to see Danny and T.J. playing with the cats. "Where are they?"

"I left them at home in their beds. Selena offered to stay with them while I visited with you."

"Selena?" Hannah had a quick moment of panic before sitting up and tossing aside the covers.

"What are you doing? You need to rest." Ethan looked toward her grandparents, hoping they would help calm her.

Instead they stood at the foot of the bed, looking as alarmed as their granddaughter.

Frank Brennan cleared his throat. "Police Chief Thompson is convinced that what happened to Hannah was no accident. When he asked for the name of anyone who might want to harm her, there was only one name that Hannah could think of. Your business partner."

"Selena?" Ethan was shaking his head. "Look, I know that she's been less than friendly, Hannah. But that's just her style. She stood by me throughout the loss of my wife and the subsequent publicity. What could she possibly gain by hurting you?"

"You said yourself that Elizabeth considered Selena to be obsessed with you, Ethan. And obsession can be a dangerous thing." Hannah handed Ethan her cell phone. "Call your house."

For a minute he stared at her blankly.

"Please, Ethan. Call home."

At her pleading, he dialed the phone and listened to it ring on and on.

He seemed perplexed. "Maybe Selena stepped out onto the deck."

"Maybe. But I have a terrible feeling about this. Oh, Ethan." Hannah got to her feet and waited for the weakness to pass. "Call Mason at the guardhouse. Ask if Selena was seen leaving."

"Leaving?" He went pale before dialing again.

"Mason? Ethan Harrison." His tone deepened. "Did you happen to see Ms. Crain leave?"

He listened in grim silence. His tone went flat. "Did you happen to notice if my boys were in the car?"

Another silence before he said, "How long ago?"

He rang off before glancing at Hannah and her grandparents. "She left nearly fifteen minutes ago. She has the boys."

Hannah reached for the phone,and when he handed it over, she dialed, listened, then said, "Boyd, this is Hannah Brennan. Selena Crain was seen by the guard at Ethan Harrison's complex driving away with his sons." She handed the phone to Ethan.

Boyd's voice could be heard booming over the line. "I went to the Harbor House hoping to interview Selena Crain. I was told she had checked out. Did she have your permission to take your sons?"

"Of course not. I left them asleep in their

beds. She had agreed to stay with them until I returned.''

''Then it's kidnapping.'' Boyd's words were clipped. ''She's probably headed for the interstate. Give me a description of her car.''

Ethan shook his head, struggling to think. ''It's a rental.''

''Good. There's only one rental agency in town. They'll have the license number. Now give me a number where you can be reached. I'll call you as soon as her car is spotted.''

''I can't just sit here. I need to be out looking for my sons.'' Ethan was fighting a rising sense of panic.

''I know you do.'' Boyd's tone was calm and deliberate. ''I have kids of my own, Mr. Harrison. I understand how you feel. But you'll just be in the way. Better to stay put until we contact you.'' He noted the number. ''You're at Hannah's place?''

''That's right.''

''Stay there. Let the guard at your complex know that I'm sending an officer to your home to have a look around. I'll also alert the state police. Trust me. This woman won't get far. As soon as she's spotted, you'll be the first to know.''

When Boyd rang off, Ethan started to pace, overcome with guilt and grief. "What was I thinking? Why didn't I see this coming?"

Hannah wanted to say something comforting, but her mind was in such turmoil all she could do was lay a hand on his arm.

He spoke in a fierce whisper, almost to himself. "All day Selena has been nagging me to agree to come back with her to Fair Harbor. She kept insisting that it was the only way we could make the Davis Corporation happy. When I refused, she became adamant. They're our biggest client. Their contract alone is worth several million a year. Without that, we'd be forced to cut back on services to other clients."

"What did she suggest you do about the boys?"

He clenched his teeth. "That was the sticking point. She had the name of a very reputable live-in nanny with excellent recommendations. I told her Danny and T.J. weren't ready for a nanny yet. And neither was I."

"I can't imagine that made her very happy."

He shook his head, and there was an edge of panic in his voice. "Come to think of it, she was furious. Then she became enraged when I said I was going to wake the boys and take them with me to your place. But a minute later she seemed to be over it, and even offered to stay with them so I wouldn't have to disturb their sleep.'' He ran his fingers through his hair and turned away to pace again. ''This is all my fault. I didn't listen to Elizabeth when she voiced her fears, and it cost her her life. Look what was done to you today. And now...my sons.''

Hannah tried to calm him. ''You said yourself that your detectives could find no flaw in Selena's alibi. Why would you suspect her when they'd cleared her?''

''Because a husband and father should have better instincts.''

''Ethan, you can't blame yourself for this.'' Hannah looked to her grandparents, who stood by helplessly.

Hannah took her grandmother's hand. ''You two should go home and try to get some rest.''

Bert shook her head. ''We'll sleep later. Right now we're staying until this is resolved.''

''But this could last...'' Hannah's head came up at the sound of footsteps on the stairs.

She turned just as the door opened. Standing in the doorway was Selena. She seemed as calm, as composed as though she'd just stopped by for a friendly visit. Except that in her hand was a very small, very lethal-looking gun.

Chapter 16

"Selena." Ethan started toward her. "Where are my sons?"

She waved the gun menacingly. "Get back."

"Not until you tell me..."

She took careful aim. "I said step back, Ethan. Stand over there with your lover. Let's see if she brings you any comfort now."

He put a hand protectively on Hannah's arm. "Is Hannah the reason for this madness?"

Selena's eyes narrowed to tiny slits. "You call it madness? How dare you demean what I feel."

Hannah's voice was oddly calm in the midst

of this volatile storm. "What do you feel, Selena?"

"Ethan and I are soul mates. I knew that the moment we met. He was the first man I'd ever known who was smarter than me. Our friends, our classmates, even our professors were in awe of his mind. When my family learned that I was forsaking them to join forces with Ethan on his fledgling business, they were horrified, until they met him. Then they understood. They agreed that we were the perfect team."

She turned to Ethan. "But then you had to go and spoil it all. Elizabeth wasn't worthy of you, Ethan. She was a distraction, keeping you from your life's work. I thought I could simply drive her away. I knew if I managed that, you'd turn to me for solace and realize how perfect we were together. But the fool wouldn't run. Instead she had a baby, and then another, and thought she could hide behind security alarms and even a gun."

"It was you?" A look of complete disbelief crossed Ethan's face. "My detectives checked your alibi, Selena. They said you were clear across town when Elizabeth was shot. There was no way you could have had time to drive to my house, kill Elizabeth and return to the client's office.''

Selena actually smiled, feeling in control again. ''You aren't the only genius on this team, Ethan. I'd spent weeks calculating every minute I would need. I drove the route between your house and our client's office dozens of times until I'd found every shortcut, every back alley that would shave time. I even allowed for traffic jams, accidents, unexpected incidents that might slow things down.

''I chose a day when I knew Elizabeth would be alone, and I told her I needed to drop off some documents for you to read. Once inside, I calmly drew my gun and told her that I'd come there to kill her and her sons.'' Selena pursed her lips. ''From everything I've read, I know that a new mother is often overwrought. With T.J. only weeks old, I expected Elizabeth to still be weak. I certainly never expected her to calmly stand her ground the way she did. Instead of hysteria, she said she'd always known I was her rival. Then she slipped a pistol from her pocket and told me the minute she'd seen my car, she'd become suspicious. Further, she told me, if I didn't leave, she wouldn't be the only one dead.''

Ethan's voice trembled with fury. ''Did you

really expect a loving mother to calmly step aside and allow you to harm her children?''

''I didn't see that she had any choice.''

Ethan's entire body was shaking with rage. ''How did you get her to go to the garage?''

''Elizabeth heard Danny calling from upstairs, where he'd been napping. She ordered me at gunpoint to leave through the garage door, thinking he wouldn't have time to see me and be afraid. As she was following me, I stepped aside and pulled her off balance. She stumbled, causing the gun to fall from her hand. I saw it as the perfect opportunity. Instead of my own gun, I used hers.'' Selena puffed with pride. ''I thought that was a touch of genius. Now it wasn't simply an unexplained murder, but rather a mystery. Was poor Elizabeth the victim of a crime or simply an overwrought new mother suffering from postpartum depression? Even the authorities couldn't agree.''

Ethan paled as the truth of his wife's horrible death dawned. ''You even robbed her of her dignity. Instead of letting the world know that she'd sacrificed her life for her sons, she was being thought of as a tragic figure. Weak and fragile and unable to cope with her life.''

Hannah wondered that she could still speak

over the fury that threatened to choke her. "Why did you spare the boys?"

"I heard a door slam nearby and thought a neighbor may have heard the gunshot. I didn't want to spoil my timetable, so I let myself out of the garage and drove away. When I'd had time to think about it, I realized that it might work to my advantage to have the boys alive. I figured Ethan would be so locked in grief, he would need my help with them in the future. Especially since his own family and friends began to distance themselves from him." She smiled. "With a little help from me."

"It seems you thought of everything."

Selena looked Hannah up and down with contempt. "Everything except the possibility that my soul mate could actually lose his heart to yet another woman so completely unworthy of him." She sneered. "A woman who…grovels in the dirt."

Hannah wasn't troubled by the insult. For now it didn't matter what Selena thought of her. What mattered was finding a way to stop her.

"If you love Ethan, how can you bear to bring him such pain?"

"What about my pain? When is it my turn to find a little happiness?" Selena's voice rose on a thread of hysteria. "I've finally realized that Ethan Harrison isn't worthy of me. He deserves to die like his wife did."

Hannah nodded. "You're angry with him."

"And with you, you slut, for stealing what was rightfully mine."

"Is that why you laced my water with poison?"

"I wanted you to suffer a long, painful death." Selena turned the gun on Frank and Bert, who had watched and listened in stunned silence. "But I think I know another way to make you suffer. The lives of these two old fools ought to be just the thing to make you beg and plead before you die. As for you—" she fixed her gaze on Ethan "—you'll get to watch your sons die. That ought to be punishment enough for the man who so callously broke my heart."

Ethan grasped the only thing that seemed to have penetrated the pain that clouded his mind. "Are you saying that Danny and T.J. aren't dead yet?"

"Not yet. But soon."

For the first time he felt a flicker of hope. If his sons were alive, he had to survive, for their sake. "Where are they?"

Selena smiled. "They're safe. For the moment."

"How can you be sure of that?"

"The younger one is asleep. I told his older brother that if he behaved, and didn't move until I returned, I'd have a wonderful surprise for him." Selena actually threw back her head and laughed as she brandished her weapon. "Isn't this a lovely surprise?"

Ethan was staring at her through narrowed eyes. "You're mad."

Her laughter died as abruptly as it had begun. "That's exactly what your wife said. But you're both wrong. I'm a woman scorned. I have a right to demand justice."

"You call murdering an innocent woman justice? And what about all these innocent people? I won't let it happen again." Ethan could feel the last thread of his temper unravel as he started across the room toward her.

"Stop." Selena pointed the gun at Ethan's chest. "I don't want to have to kill you first, Ethan. You have to die last, so that your pain is greater."

"Sorry to spoil your timetable." Almost blind with rage, he lunged and drove her back against the door.

As they came together, a single shot echoed through the room, and both Ethan and Selena seemed to stiffen before they fell to the floor in a heap.

"Ethan. No." Hannah saw the pistol fall from Selena's hand and skid across the floor. Picking it up, she waded in to pull Ethan and Selena apart.

The minute Selena was free of Ethan's weight, she regained her footing and kicked viciously at Hannah, sending her sprawling. Then she was on her like a wild creature scenting blood.

"This is all your fault." Selena's arm swung in an arc. Before she could connect with flesh, Hannah's fingers closed around her wrist.

Selena looked shocked at the strength in Hannah's grasp. Tears sprang to her eyes as, in one quick move, Hannah flipped her over and pinned her, all the while squeezing the bones of her wrist.

Through clenched teeth Hannah pressed the pistol to Selena's head. "If you were looking for an easy target, you made a big mistake. Just the way you did when you misjudged a mother's love."

Selena went very still, awaiting the sound of

another gunshot. She closed her eyes. "Go ahead. Kill me."

"It's tempting. But far too easy. I want you to suffer a long, humiliating trial instead, during which you can give back Elizabeth Harrison her good name." Hannah scrambled to her feet. "I want you to tell the world that Elizabeth Harrison was a hero for sacrificing her life for her sons. I want you to tell the world that Ethan Harrison had no hand in the hideous thing you did."

Hannah tossed the gun to her grandfather. "Watch her, Poppie. And don't hesitate to shoot if she moves."

As Frank took up a position over Selena, Hannah hurried to Ethan's side.

Seeing the blood staining his shirt, she clutched at him, cradling him in her arms. "Oh, Ethan, where were you hit?"

He managed a weak smile as he stared at the torn flesh of his arm. "I think the bullet passed clear through."

"Thank heaven." She was already tearing the sleeve of his shirt and tying it around the wound to stem the flow of blood while Bert, ever efficient, returned from the bathroom with a wet cloth.

They looked up when the door was roughly

kicked open and Chief Boyd Thompson rushed in, pistol drawn. He took in the scene before him, then knelt to handcuff Selena before handing her to a fellow officer.

As she was being led away, Frank Brennan said, "She admitted that she killed Elizabeth Harrison and had planned to kill all of us, as well."

Boyd gave him a grim smile. "I'd hate to be her defense attorney, knowing she has one of the finest judges in the country as a witness to her confession."

"My sons…" Ethan began, but stopped when Boyd held up a hand.

"They're safe and sound and in the squad car with two of my officers."

"Where were they?"

"Downstairs, in Ms. Crain's rental car." He glanced at Ethan's bloody shirt. "I'll phone for an ambulance, Mr. Harrison."

Ethan shook his head. "I don't need one. Right now I just want to hold my sons."

Boyd Thompson nodded. "I'll have them brought up." He spoke into his phone. Minutes later two burly officers entered, each holding one of the boys.

T.J.'s head was cradled on an officer's shoulder. When Hannah reached out for him, he snuggled into her arms, yawned and closed his eyes.

"Daddy." The minute he was set down, Danny danced across the room and into his father's waiting arms. Seeing the blood he said, "Did you cut yourself?"

"I guess I did. But I'm fine, now that you're here."

"I did what Selena said. I didn't move the whole time she was gone. Now can I have my surprise?"

Ethan closed his eyes on a wave of relief. "Oh, yes, Danny. I think my good boy deserves the best surprise of all." He smoothed the blond hair from his son's forehead and stared down into his eyes. "If you could have anything in the world, what would it be?"

"Anything in the whole world?" Danny's eyes grew round.

"Anything, son."

The little boy glanced shyly at Hannah, holding his little brother, then turned to stare into his father's eyes. "I know we've got a mommy in heaven. But could Hannah be our mommy here on earth?"

Ethan looked into his son's eyes before walking over to Hannah. "Why don't you ask her?"

Danny nodded. "Hannah, would you be our mommy?"

T.J., waking at that moment, echoed, "Mommy?" He looked up at Hannah with those big, trusting eyes, and she felt her heart nearly explode with happiness.

"I can't think of anything I'd like more. But I think we need to hear from your daddy."

"You mean, 'cause you'd be his mommy, too?" the little boy asked.

Ethan found himself laughing. Despite all the horror they'd been through, all the pain, all the fear, his heart was suddenly lighter than air. "No, Danny. She'd be my wife." He reached out to touch a hand to her cheek. "I know it's a lot to ask, Hannah, but would you consider it? Being my wife and their mommy?"

She met his eyes. Her own sparked with humor. "I'm awfully tempted."

Danny looked from one to the other, then took his father's face in his chubby hands and said, "I know how you can get Hannah to say yes, Daddy."

"How?"

"You should offer to take her to the Dairy Devil for hot dogs."

"You think the hot dogs will do it?"

"Not the hot dogs," Danny said solemnly. "You have to carve our initials and Hannah's in the table. Then the whole town will know that she's our girlfriend."

"Girlfwend," T.J. echoed, half-asleep.

Ethan bit back a smile. "That's pretty serious stuff."

Danny nodded. "Ask her, Daddy. If she says yes to the Dairy Devil, she'll say yes to being our wife."

"My wife," Ethan corrected.

"Wife," T.J. echoed before yawning again.

"I think it's too late to go to the Dairy Devil tonight." Hannah saw her grandparents watching and listening with matching smiles. "But maybe tomorrow, after we all have a good night's sleep, we could pick up Bert and Poppie and we could all go for hot dogs and milkshakes and carve our initials."

Danny rubbed at his eyes. "And then the whole town will know we belong together."

"That's right, son. We do belong together." Ethan met Hannah's eyes and felt the thrill all the way to his soul. "It was fate that brought us here. And fate that brought you into our lives, Hannah. I want the whole town to know that we belong together."

"Why stop with the whole town?" Hannah's laughter rang on the air. "I think the whole world ought to know."

"Is that a yes?"

She leaned close to brush her mouth over his. "How can I resist being your garden angel for a lifetime?"

Frank Brennan cleared his throat, causing Ethan and Hannah to glance over with matching looks of guilt.

"It's time Bert and I headed home."

Still holding T.J., Hannah crossed the room to press a kiss to each of their cheeks. "What would I do without you?"

Ethan stood beside her and offered his handshake. "There aren't enough words to thank you for all you've done. You welcomed us into your home, even when you knew nothing about us."

"We knew enough." Frank clapped a hand on Ethan's shoulder. "Our granddaughter has always had very good taste."

Bert stood on tiptoe to press a kiss to Ethan's cheek. "Take very good care of her heart, young man, because it's going to be yours for a lifetime."

When they were gone, Ethan turned to Hannah. The look in his eyes, so hot and fierce, had her heart tripping over itself. "I can't believe my good fortune, Hannah. I never thought I could be this happy."

She settled T.J. into one side of her bed, then lifted a sleeping Danny from his arms and laid him beside his brother, before taking Ethan's hand and leading him toward the balcony.

The midnight sky was awash with stars.

She reached up and wrapped her arms around his neck, brushing his lips with soft, butterfly kisses.

"My beautiful, beguiling garden angel. I believe we'll need more than one lifetime for all the love we're about to share."

At the purr in his throat she sighed. "All right. How about an eternity together?"

"That's much better."

"I agree." Then, because words seemed inadequate, she began to show him, with long slow kisses, all the feelings of love that were in her heart.

*   *   *   *   *

If you enjoyed Hannah's story,
be sure to look for
sister Courtney's book

VENDETTA,

coming next month from
Silhouette Intimate Moments.
Turn the page for a sneak preview...

Chapter 1

"It has to be something really unique." Prentice Osborn took another turn around Courtney Brennan's gift shop, Treasures. "I want to give it to Carrie tonight when I ask her..." He stopped abruptly when he realized what he'd almost revealed and glanced over quickly at the only other patron in the shop, Wade Bentley, the mayor of Devil's Cove, who was being assisted by Kendra Crowley, the high school graduate Courtney had hired to help in the shop for the summer. The mayor seemed to be busy examining a display of pretty painted glassware on the far side of the room. "Not a word, Courtney."

"My lips are sealed." Though she didn't crack a smile, the glint of humor in Courtney's eyes gave her away. The romance between Prentice, from one of Devil Cove's wealthiest families, and Carrie Lester, who worked in the Daisy Diner, was the worst kept secret in town. It was impossible not to notice Prentice hanging around the diner for hours while Carrie worked her shift, just so he could walk her home.

At first, whenever they went out to dinner, they'd taken along his mentally challenged brother, Will, and Carrie's daughter, Jenny. Lately they'd been seen without their chaperones, lingering over late-night seafood and the world's best cheesecake at The Pier, one of Devil Cove's finest restaurants.

"How about this?" Courtney held up a hand-painted gargoyle.

"I said unique, not ugly."

"I think it's adorable. Knowing Carrie, she'd agree."

He gave it a closer appraisal. "Do you really think Carrie would like something like that?"

"Absolutely. Look." Courtney held it up to the window. "The artist gave it a secret." Light spilled through, revealing a tiny heart that could only be seen when it was turned a certain way.

"Wow." Prentice took it from Courtney's hand and turned this way and that, watching the heart appear and disappear. Just looking at it had him grinning.

He seemed to be reconsidering. "It's different, all right. I'm just not sure it's special enough. How will I know if she really likes it or if she's just humoring me?"

Courtney gave her childhood friend a gentle smile. "Prentice, Carrie is going to love anything you buy for her."

"Is it that obvious?" He actually blushed, a trait that Courtney found endearing.

"It is." She patted his arm. "But your secret is safe with me."

Prentice sighed before handing over the gargoyle. "All right. Wrap it up. I'm going to give it to her tonight after dinner. Right before I pop the big question."

Courtney cushioned the little sculpture in tissue before fitting it into one of the gold-and-silver boxes that bore the name Treasures on the lid. That, in turn, was tucked into a handled bag with the same gold-and-silver design. The bags had become such a fashion statement, they were the favorite totes of many of the town's tourists and year-round residents.

Courtney handed him his credit card and receipt along with the bag. ''Good luck, Prentice.''

''Thanks.'' He paused. ''You've got a great shop here, Courtney. I know I'm not the only one in town who's glad you came home. You've added a lot of class to Devil's Cove.''

''Thanks, Prentice. Good night.'' She watched as he walked outside, then turned to where the mayor was still studying the glassware.

''See anything you like, Wade?'' Courtney glanced at her watch, eager to close up shop. She'd been here since her first delivery at nine o'clock, and it was now well past the dinner hour.

The mayor shrugged and ambled toward the counter, carrying a pair of hand-painted candlesticks. ''Thinking about buying these. Your young assistant tells me they're all the rage.''

''They're beautiful. I don't believe I've ever seen you in Treasures before, Wade.''

He smiled, showing white, even teeth in a handsome, tanned face. In his early forties, he still ran the annual summer marathon and routinely beat runners years younger.

The Bentley family had been involved in politics in the state since Wade's father, Dade Bentley, had been governor. The name alone was enough to guarantee recognition wherever he went. When Wade had decided to make his mark in the town of Devil's Cove, he'd found little competition. There was talk that he might be considering a run for the state senate in the next year. With his family history, his good looks and winning way with people, it was rumored that he might even use that as a stepping stone to Washington.

Courtney began carefully wrapping the candlesticks before placing them in a bag.

He handed over his charge card. "The city clerk tells me you're interested in buying the Colby cottage."

Courtney smiled. "That's right. I guess there's not much that goes on in this town that you don't know about, Wade."

He returned the smile before signing the sales slip. "Not much. What're you planning on doing with it? Not tearing it down, I hope."

"I'd live there and enlarge my shop, maybe turn the upstairs where I'm living now into an art gallery."

He glanced around. "A fine idea, Courtney. You've got a really nice place here. I guess the Colby cottage would be a nice addition to your holdings." He turned away. "Good night."

"'Night, Wade."

As soon as he was gone, Kendra walked behind the counter and retrieved her denim bag from a locked cabinet. Her hair, bright orange spikes, framed a heart-shaped face made sultry by dark, sooty eyelids and a mouth outlined in deep purple. She bought all her clothes from a nearby resale shop, the more outrageous the better. Today she wore a shapeless fringed sack dress that might have been popular in the seventies, topped by a fitted denim vest painted with old peace signs. She'd confided to Courtney that she was only going on to college in the fall to please her father. Her real goal was to own her own retail shop.

"Geez," she huffed as she slung her bag over her shoulder. "I thought he'd never leave."

"Hey, a sale's a sale. Besides, it doesn't hurt to have the town's mayor shopping here. And he bought some very expensive candlesticks."

"Yeah. I'm not complaining. But he took long enough." Kendra started toward the door where her boyfriend, sporting teal spiked hair and a tie-dyed T-shirt, was waiting. "See you tomorrow."

"Thanks, Kendra. And thanks for steering the mayor toward that glassware."

"No problem."

Courtney followed the young woman to the door and locked it behind her before flipping over the little sign, indicating the time the shop would be opened in the morning. She picked up a clutch of mail before heading for the back room and the stairs that led to her apartment above the shop.

Once there, she kicked off her shoes and poured herself an iced tea before sorting through the mail. Except for the usual bills, the letter she'd been hoping for was conspicuously absent.

In the time she'd been back, Courtney had turned this tiny shop into the talk of the town. Though she'd originally intended to stay only long enough to mend her heartache, she'd discovered something about her hometown. There was as much charm in the little town of Devil's Cove as there was in Milan or Paris. And the number of local artists and artisans continued to surprise her. The quality of their workmanship was equal to or better than their European counterparts.

Courtney had never regretted coming home. Though she'd once thought of it as an admission of defeat, she now realized that this town and its people had always held a special place in her heart. The bond she had with her family was stronger than ever. And the thought of being close to her grandparents in their sunset years gave her such pleasure. Not that Bert and Poppie were old. At least not in Courtney's eyes. Despite their ages, they were the youngest-at-heart people she knew.

She walked to the balcony and looked out at the cottage that stood behind her place. Since Sarah Colby's death, Courtney had begun keeping a close eye on the empty cottage. It saddened her to see no gardens planted. No vines drifting from the window boxes that Sarah had so lovingly painted and planted each year.

The vacant cottage was apparently an object of some interest. Several times Courtney had seen beams of light being played along the darkened building. Fearing vandalism, she'd asked Police Chief Boyd Thompson to dispatch a scout car to the location. Now the police routinely drove by the cottage several times a week.

Courtney wondered how long it would take to hear from the law firm in Boston. Knowing how slowly these things moved through the courts, Courtney couldn't hold back the dreams she'd begun weaving. By moving into the cottage, she could double the space of her shop. And because the property behind the Colby cottage ran right down to the water's edge, she could keep her boat there. She could already picture the little paved courtyard she was planning between the shop and the cottage, ringed with gardens, which would make the perfect showcase for the garden sculptures she'd begun accumulating from several local artists.

She was just turning away when she caught sight of a shadowy figure darting across the yard. While she watched, the figure paused at the door to the cottage and began turning the knob.

She was across the room in seconds, dashing barefoot down the stairs and across the yard while she dialed the emergency number on her cell phone.

''You there.'' She struggled for breath. ''Stop right where you are.''

The figure, halfway across the threshold, froze, before turning. At first glance she sucked in a breath. The man facing her was so tall she had to tilt her head to see his eyes. In the moonlight they appeared as icy as the waters of Lake Michigan in winter, and were narrowed on her with a challenging look.

''Is there a problem?'' His voice matched his eyes. Frigid. Tinged with arrogance.

''There will be if you try to break in there.''

Now she had his full attention.

His tone cooled by degrees. "What business is it of yours where I go?"

"I've been watching out for this property since the owner died."

"I see. And you would be...?"

"Courtney Brennan."

"Brennan?" He looked at her with new interest. "I'm Blair Colby. Sarah's nephew." He picked up a duffel lying near his feet. "I was told by Hibner and Sloan that you contacted them about buying the place."

"Oh." Her relief was evident in the smile that touched her mouth. "You've come to discuss the terms. Would you like to come over to my place and we can talk? That's my shop, and I live above it."

He barely flicked a glance in her direction. "Sorry to mislead you. I didn't come to sell. I'll be staying here, at least for the summer."

"I see." Her heart fell. "Then I'm sorry to have bothered you."

"No bother."

They both looked up as a police cruiser came to a screeching halt and a burly figure in uniform strode toward them.

"Trouble, Courtney?"

"I'm sorry, Boyd. I overreacted. This is

Sarah's nephew, Blair Colby. This is our police chief, Boyd Thompson.''

''Chief.'' Blair offered a handshake. ''Nice to see everyone looking out for my aunt's place.''

Boyd put his hands on his hips. ''You got some ID?''

A flicker of annoyance crossed Blair's face as he once again dropped his duffel before reaching into his back pocket and removing a wallet. Flipping it open, he held it up while the police officer studied it in the beam of his flashlight.

''Okay.'' Boyd nodded. ''Can't be too careful. Courtney here has scared off intruders a couple of times since your aunt's death.''

''Intruders?'' Blair turned to her in surprise.

The police chief answered for her. ''Probably just teens intent on mischief. But everybody here looks out for everybody else.'' He switched off his flashlight and hooked it on to his belt before offering a handshake. ''Welcome to Devil's Cove, Mr. Colby.''

''Thanks.'' Blair returned the handshake.

''You plan on staying, or just here to go over your aunt's things?''

''I'll be here at least for the summer.''

''I see.'' Boyd looked up at the voice squawking over the squad car's radio. "I'd better answer that call."

As he strolled away, Blair turned to Courtney. "Any more questions?"

"Sorry. I thought it best to err on the side of caution."

"You're right, of course. Thanks for keeping an eye on my aunt's place. But now, if you'll excuse me, it's been a long day." Deliberately turning his back on Courtney, he picked up his duffel and stepped inside, closing the door in her face.

Feeling more than a little foolish, she picked her way over the lawn and climbed the stairs to her apartment. From her balcony she could see the lights winking on in the windows of the Colby cottage. It seemed strange to think of someone being there. Strange and sad.

She'd been a fool to allow herself to begin thinking of it as hers. Once again, it would seem, all her carefully laid plans had been thwarted by a man. From the little she'd seen of him, an arrogant man, as well.

No big deal, she thought with a sigh. The story of her life.

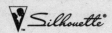

If you enjoyed what you just read,
then we've got an offer you can't resist!

Take 2 bestselling love stories FREE!
Plus get a FREE surprise gift!

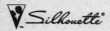
Silhouette®

INTIMATE MOMENTS™

From reader favorite
SARA ORWIG

Bring on the Night
(Silhouette Intimate Moments, #1298)

With a ranch in Stallion Pass, Jonah Whitewolf
inherited a mysterious danger—a threatening
enemy with a vendetta against him. When he
runs into his ex-wife, Kate Valentini, in town,
he comes face-to-face with the secret she's kept—
the son he never knew. With the truth revealed,
Jonah must put his life in peril to protect his
ranch and his family from jeopardy. But can he
face the greatest risk of all and give himself up
to love a second time around?

STALLION PASS:
TEXAS KNIGHTS

*Where the only cure for those hot and sultry
Lone Star Days are some sexy-as-all-get-out
Texas Knights!*

Available June 2004 at your favorite retail outlet.

INTIMATE MOMENTS

SIMCNM0504